A LINE IN THE SAND

Jack McClean #1

Paul Mageen

Paul Mageen

Cover photo arched gateway in the Alameda Malaga copyright Paul Mageen 2021

FOREWORD

Jack McClean was a real person who played for Bradford Northern with my dad in the fifties. Rugby league is played by hard men who don't take a backward step.
I have borrowed Jack's name and created a fictional character, there is no other relationship.

CHAPTER 1

Mack took a deep breath. He knew how this was going to end. Jack McClean was standing in front of a desk. Behind the desk was a thug. A proper Neanderthal. A Silverback. Shaven headed (where he wasn't bald), a tattoo saying "Lucifer" on his neck. An arm full of tribal art (if you can call a rape scene tribal art) the genuine three roll neck to go with the barrel chest and the bigger barrel belly. A gold front tooth with inset diamond. Hands like meat shovels with sausage fingers. Simple dots on each finger, probably self-administered before he could afford a professional artist. This guy did need professional help, which was why Mack was there. Mack was intelligent in the real academic way. He was also smart in the street savvy way. Mack was a go-to man, he worked between gangs. People who would rather kill each other used Mack as a fixer and go-between. He had worked his way into gangland by pure aggression.

The sausage fingers belonging to Lee Handforth

had strangled people, stabbed people, smashed glasses and bottles in people's faces, they had handled all sorts of drugs and they had been the most dangerous sausage fingers in Manchester for many years. The owner of the fingers and the meat shovel hands they were attached to had no conscience. He was incapable of feeling beyond the results of his actions and the results of his actions usually made him more money.

Longsight in Manchester was his former stomping ground and he had done plenty of stomping. An area where survival was the only goal in life; rows of smelly bedsits and smelly people. The great unwashed. Drug use and violence were part of the rich tapestry of the area and it was here where Lee Handforth dished out both in equal measure. He had rarely attended school unless dragged there by a social worker, only to walk straight back out again. His only education was gained on deprived streets and old copies of the 'Sun' newspaper. He had learned that kindness wasn't mistaken for softness. Neither existed in Longsight. The only way to earn money was illegally and he had learned from local petty thieves, drug dealers and loan collectors.

People were desperate. For money, for cigs, for drugs, for booze, for sex. They would borrow money at extortionate rates to make it to the end of the week or the month and then find that they could not make the repayment which then rose to an even more unaffordable level. It wasn't just a downward spiral; it was a nosedive into oblivion. Lee Handforth used to beat them senseless, take their only belongings and then come back the next week and do it again. It was by no means unusual to find the poor individual dead and already stinking. No matter, the loan shark had made his money back with profit weeks ago; on to the next address.

In this environment Lee Handforth had thrived and lived long enough to work his way inside the circle to eventually establish his own patch of misery. Further expansion of his operations involved stepping onto rival territories. Power struggles ensued and basically the most vicious scumbag usually won the day. He would rely on employing other, equally vicious scumbags. There was no shortage of underlings who had trod a similar path and were making their way in evil land. There was no way out; no way to move into mainstream society and earn an honest crust. Handforth could not imagine working for three hundred quid a week with a mortgage and kids and such. He already had kids, at least three and he paid fuck all to the mothers. He might slip them a wrap of what they needed now and then and to Handforth that was the entire acknowledgement he needed to these scruffy little urchins. He couldn't survive forever though. Even Lee Handforth knew this; he was far from stupid. There was always some ambitious violent motherfucker such as he had once been and eventually his luck would run out. So he ran.

So it happened that, in this case, the uncrowned King of Marbella needed to communicate with a Ukrainian gang of black evilness. Nobody in his position would appear in the flesh in the other gang's manor.

The desk, and hence the office, was above a bar in a backstreet of Puerto Banús on the Costa del Sol on Spain's southern coast. Handforth was the gang leader, a pimp, a drug baron. The nastiest of the nasties. His reputation was well earned. UK Police had him down for at least seven murders without sufficient evidence (people did not give evidence against Lee Handforth). However that was several years ago. Nowadays Handforth survived on an atmosphere of fear and intimidation plus an entourage of sycophants and lackeys. In this case, Handforth was attended by two henchmen (makes him sound like a Bond villain) one of which was clearly a heroin addict and looked more like Skeletor than He-Man. The other was a steroid filled hulk trying his best to imitate the Big Man. These were the bottom feeding wankers who had no education, no chance of being a part of normal society, had never been outside their own circle of evil and had grabbed their only opportunity to survive by hanging onto the coat tails of somebody who knew how to operate in this world and could keep them supplied with money and drugs.

So what was Mack doing there? Handforth been introduced to him as Mack had earned himself a reputation of getting the job done in a "no questions asked" kind of way. We'll see later how this happened; for now just run with it. I suppose discretion is the word we are looking for. For the fees Mack commanded, Mack was good and he was expensive. This was because he was a specialist in violence. OK, let's not beat around the bush; Mack would go to any lengths to get the job done. Sometimes that meant people getting hurt. Alright, not so much hurt as seriously fucking injured. However, none of these losers had a clue about Mack's hidden agenda. How he could make himself look like the ideal tool to a gangland shitbag when all he was doing was pretending to be the ideal man for the job. He was, in fact, the right man for the job it's just that the job wasn't what the thug thought it was. Well, let's just say that they weren't singing from the same hymn sheet.

Jack Mclean was 32 years old. Six foot two and knocking on seventeen and a half stone. This was well proportioned as, unlike the fat fucker in front of him, Mack kept himself in shape. In his teens and early twenties he had studied the martial arts. He was a third Dan Black Belt in Bushinkai karate, a street-fighting style developed in the East End of London. He was also a Black Belt in Taekwondo specialising in breaking boards and blocks. He had taken up body building about ten years ago but downgraded that to heavy work outs to avoid becoming too big and too immobile. You see, mobility was everything to Mack. He had developed his hand and foot speed to incredible effect. If he hit you, you rarely saw it coming. The problem was you wouldn't see the next one coming either. And the worst thing was, for the recipient, every blow was like a sledge hammer. He would take somebody out in seconds without the need to increase his breathing. The thing was though, despite this ability, he was not a bully and never intimidated anyone. His demeanour was generally laid back. He was outwardly friendly, and genuinely so. He enjoyed a pint (not to excess) and mixed well. There was only one downside to being amiable and approachable. Occasionally some idiot would have a beer too many and think it was a good idea to come the "hard man" either towards Mack or in his company. We will come to that later as well.

Lee Handforth was in the process of importing 5 kilos of grade "A" heroin from Morocco. It was actually 3 kilos but it would end up at 5 kilos when Handforth had finished with it. Word was that a bunch of Ukrainian types from Estepona were interested in the shipment, only because Handforth knew that this was their business and would need a regular supply.. Handforth needed to know if there was a danger of hijack in the process; the value of this shipment was in the six figure bracket and he needed to ensure that the drugs went one way and the money the other in safety.. "Listen, I need you to make contact with these fucking ruskies and work out how they want this to go down". Mack thought about this. "It won't be easy turning up out of the blue and getting them to deal with me." "I don't give a fuck, for the money I'm paying you I don't care if you have to take one up the arse to get in there" "Yeah, well that won't be happening" Mack replied. "You'll just have to trust me to set the deal up in my own way". This was the part where these conversations never went well. Mack had been in this situation many times. He had been in the presence of these monsters and knew that they could not resist a threat. It was in their nature, in their bloodstream; it was how they had achieved the notoriety they enjoyed. And it was inevitable now. "I'm not going to tell you this again". Actually, that is what the fat bastard started to say. In reality he only got so far as "I'm not going....." It was the look on his face that did it. The top lip drawn back, the snarling look. Mack had already decided what would happen in this situation. As I said, he was a bright lad and he had been in this situation before. At the moment the thug put on the face and opened his mouth Mack turned and smashed henchman #1 (the steroid abuser) in the face, using his first two knuckles to drive the bridge of his nose back into his skull. In a split second he delivered a driving kick with the heel of his shoe (he never wore trainers) through the jaw of the Skeletor lookalike. This instantly took the useless skinny twat out of the equation whilst ensuring a visit to the dentist. As the Buster Bloodvessel* lookalike attempted to gain his feet. Mack simply drove a lightning strike through his jawbone and dropped him like a sack of the proverbial. This took about three seconds, in which time Handforth has only just started to open the drawer in front of him. Clearly this would contain something dangerous so Mack simply kicked the front of the desk and pinned the fat arsehole against the wall. At this point the expression on Handforth's face had changed from one of menace to one of mixed surprise and panic. Mack placed his hands on the front of the desk and stated in a calm voice "Don't threaten me ever again" He slowly pulled the desk away allowing Handforth some room to move. "I've made my point, but be really careful what you do next". Handforth was an old hand at violence, he simply smiled and said "Fuck me you're a handy cunt aren't you?" A smile also reached Mack's face "I hope we haven't got off to a bad start?" Handforth replied "I think we have a better understanding. Daft as it may seem, I am now thinking you may be just the man for the job" "Gaz said you were worth looking at" We'll find out about Gaz later.

Mack thought it better to vacate the premises at this point and said "I only require half my fee in cash now and I can get on with the job". He could see the initial hesitation in Handforth's face but he immediately relaxed and got up to open a safe recessed in the wall. Counting out two thousand euros in one thousand bundles Handforth looked at Mack. "This deal is worth a lot of dough. If you get this done there might be a little bonus for you". The two idiots on the floor were

just starting to groan as Mack closed the door behind him.

This was the biggest job that Mack had taken on to date. Not the gangland connection, no; it was the fact that he was dead set on destroying two illegal class 'A' drug dealing operations. Misleading two vicious deadly gangs by pretending he was something he wasn't and gaining the trust of evil killers was Mack's mission. As we get to know Mack we will see how he was changed. From a respected member of the community, a highly skilled sportsman, a genuinely nice bloke. Changed so much that he was quite able to dish out whatever he needed to to make it look as if he was also of the criminal classes.

Living and working on the Costa del Sol was to give him access to drug trade routes, high volume importers, and evil scum sucking fuckers who cared not one jot what effect their business operations had in wider society. How people's lives could be affected by one wrong turn, a chance encounter, a dodgy acquaintance or simply being in the wrong place at the wrong time. Mack was once in the wrong place at the wrong time. That was the reason he was doing what he was doing now and why fucking horrible bastards were now going to suffer the ultimate punishment. So let's get on with it shall we?

*Buster Bloodvessel was the lead singer with the seventies ska group Bad Manners and was a bit portly to say the least.

CHAPTER 2

"Are you still here?"

Mack was heading down the A7 in his M5. A brilliant sun was shining through wispy clouds and his air-con system was dealing with the heat. His destination was Estepona on the Costa del Sol. Estepona was one of the more southerly resorts that could call itself a Costa del Sol destination. A middle sized town with a pleasure boat harbour and a promenade lined with bars and restaurants. Pretty much like many others in Spain or Greece or Italy. These resort towns just about designed themselves. Promenade and harbour with the majority of tourist bars, restaurants and hotels. Moving back a street or two you find more bars and restaurants and smaller hotels and then moving into a more commercial centre with shops and department stores. Further inland you can find the urbanisations built in the nineties and noughties to accommodate the boom expansion of the Costa del Sol. Thousands of apartment blocks, three stories high in complexes with individual Spanish names and even more alongside golf courses up and down the coast. Estepona was nearer to Gibraltar than Málaga so access by air was a choice. You could also choose to fly Ryanair to Jerez if you were resident with a car.

Lee Handforth had informed him that the gang which was interested in the heroin shipment frequented an English pub called the Caribbean Mermaid. These were the jobs that Mack disliked the most. He had no inside knowledge of the gang and needed to gain the confidence of the boss, whoever that was. There was another insurmountable problem. He was English. The gang known locally as TCF (few people knew what it stood for) were notorious drug dealers, human traffickers, enforcers of territory and generally low life arseholes looking to make money in any illegitimate way.

Mack's MP3 player was hooked into the car's music system and playing "The Snake" by Al Wilson, an old Northern Soul hit. Those who know the song will know it tells of misplaced trust and betrayal. Rather apt thought Mack. His music tastes were eclectic but centred mainly on black music of various eras. Northern Soul, Tamla, Reggae and modern jazz were his main preferences with Northern Soul and its driving beat being his passion. The northern clubs that kept the music alive used to be regular haunts for him and he was fit and agile enough to enjoy the unique and energetic dance styles that still persisted.

Leaving San Pedro Alcántara under the Marbella

arch and passing Benhavís Mack dwelled on the lines of bars and restaurants, wondering how they all made a living. Actually he knew that few of them did. There simply weren't enough locals and tourists to go round. Some bars had good owners who generated a good local expat trade with a few golf tourists to make up the numbers. Others were willing to accept a few lowlife losers that were attracted to the easier pace of life on the coast. Such bars didn't last long as the losers would always encourage the owner to allow them to run up a tab; effectively drinking for free. When the tab reached a certain level the owner would consider his options. Refuse to serve them any more drink and he would never see them again, he could set up a payment plan or limit the supply. It didn't really matter either way; the scum had no money anyway and even lower moral standards. They would simply move on to another soft touch and start again. Mack understood these environments. This is why he had taken it upon himself to be more than equal to the nastiest of the scumbags he had to deal with. As careful as you could be these dickheads always found a way to intimidate you. As I said before, we'll come to that (we already had a small glimpse). In general Mack had no fear of even the worst of the thug community. He understood the mentality. He also understood the problems a lot of these kids had had in their upbringings. Most of them had needed to fight to survive. They had needed to steal to eat and they had needed to lie to whichever parent (if any) they had. They never had two. He also knew that; among these gangs were a few brighter models; kids that had no chance of an academic education, but learned "Street" quickly and thrived among the criminal classes. These were usually the ones that Mack dealt with. Pulling off the A7 onto the Estepona slip road Mack could see the Sierra Bermeja mountains to his right and the glistening Mediterranean to his left. From Marbella you entered Estepona from the west and drove down the *paseo maritimo* or promenade alongside the beach. Most of the Costa towns had built underground carparks during the boom times in the 'noughties' and Mack entered one of these, picking up his ticket at the entry barrier. As in most Costa carparks you paid for time parked on exit. Coming out into the bright midday sun Mack donned his Rayban shades and headed for a nearby tapas bar. He didn't speak fluent Spanish (it was a work in progress) but he could get by in bars and cafes as well as everyday 'good mornings' and such. Mack preferred the light lunches provided by the traditional tapas bars and ordered a mixture of meatballs, anchovies in vinegar and a Russian salad. These were regular fare for Mack and he knew their Spanish names, *albóndigas, boquerones en vinagre, ensaladilla rusa.* Just a sparkling water would be suitable for lunch; very refreshing with ice and a slice of lemon. Duly replenished Mack wandered into a tired looking bar across the road with a view to check out the social makeup of the local community. In his experience, most areas where gangs thrived were quite similar. Genuine locals tolerated and/or ignored the nasties. They were not intimidated and presented no threat. This generally gave them freedom to exist among the gang community and they also knew the unwritten rules. You didn't see anything, you didn't know anybody's name and even if you did you absolutely never said anything to the *Policia*. Puerto Banús had its share of Ukrainian and Russian thugs and they were creeping into Estepona where the competition was less. Ordering a Diet Coke Mack sat at a table in the corner trying to look uninterested but also trying to take in the scene. He knew he was in gang territory but even he was unprepared for the speed in which he was approached. "You not from here?" Mack knew as soon as he opened his mouth it would be only too obvious that he wasn't. In this instance he thought he would test the resolve of the dickhead and simply ignored him. "Oy you!" Mack feigned surprise and pretended to jump. "Sorry! I didn't realize you were talking to me". The thug was unmoved, he had the typical Slavic chiselled features; half shaven with that grey complexion that looked as if he still lived in a cold country; he obviously didn't get out much. Mack shouldn't have been surprised but he was always amazed at the balls these twats had. Mack wasn't massive but he was clearly a prime physical specimen. He wasn't covered in scars, tattoos and didn't have a shaved head. Therefore he didn't present an instant "don't mess" impression. "I was just passing and fancied a quick drink, if that's ok with you?" His tone wasn't threatening or facetious. "I don't like look of you so maybe fuck off alright?" the thug's tone was threatening. Mack just shrugged "whatever, I'll be off when I've supped this. Don't like this pub any-way". "Don't take much time" the thug slunk away to his corner. Mack sipped his drink and continued to observe. The thug was with two other foreign lowlifes stood in the corner speaking in their own language which was mumbo jumbo to Mack. In a couple of minutes Mack's prayers were answered. The gobshite put his beer down and headed in the direction of the servicios. Mack checked that his buddies were ignoring him and headed in the same direction. As he stood at the urinal the thug glanced behind him and noticed Mack coming in. "Why you still here?" Was want he intended to say but as we know by now Mack didn't let him get past "why y....." before he launched a side kick into the side of his temple. The thug still had hold of his dick and fell forwards banging into the ur-inal. Without having chance to replace his man-hood the arsehole immediately went for his pockets, clearly with the intention of pulling out a blade. Mack wanted this one to get the full treat-ment and stepped back giving the idiot enough time to pull a flick knife and release the blade. Mack smiled at him and said "Just tell me which eye you want me to stick that fucking thing into?". The thug sneered "You should left when you had chance". With this he lunged at Mack with the knife. Mack deftly sidestepped the attack and grabbed the thug's wrist, twisting at the same time and placing him in an arm lock which creased his face in pain. "I kill you, let go!". Mack simply said calmly in his ear "Let me tell you what's going to happen now you fucking piece of shit. Firstly I'm going to break your arm. Then I'm going to take the useless limb and make you stab yourself in your left eye. Then I'm going to kick seven shades of shit out of you. And just for good measure, if you survive this, you had better leave town because if I ever see you again I will put you in a wheelchair." Mack said this in a menacing way but in such a fashion that the thug knew he was fucked and started to plead. "Let me go or I kill you!" The idiot's English was clearly limited. Mack simply continued to twist on the arm with the knife in it. The arsehole would have screamed if he hadn't fainted with the pain as the tendons started to snap. With the elbow dislocated Mack let him drop to the floor. Good to his word Mack took hold of the arm just as the thug was starting to stir. He opened his eyes just in time to see the blade poised above his left eye. He closed his eyes tightly hoping this would be enough but to no avail. Mack pushed on the arm and the blade pierced the eyeball stopping only at the back of the eye socket. The useless twat had fainted again so Mack proceeded to stamp on his face until it was a bloody pulp. As Mack walked out of the pub the once brave soul was still laid in piss with a dislocated elbow, a knife sticking in his eye, a mashed up face and his dick hanging out.

In common with many Spanish bars there was a front entrance and a back door as well. Mack made a hasty retreat out of the back door and was out of sight in seconds. The fuckwits in the bar would find their henchman in a right state in the toilet and wonder what the fuck had gone on. Only the idiot in the toilet had spoken to Mack believing that he was among his cronies and could get away with threatening anyone with impunity. It was such a common factor among the scum classes that they thought that they were untouchable. So arrogant had they become that they enjoyed the old 'who are you looking at' attitude and employed it incessantly. Well surprise surprise; things had changed.

Mack wandered around until he spotted the Caribbean Mermaid and sat down on the terrace of the bar across the road and ordered a *café con leche* the strong Spanish coffee he enjoyed probably too much.

The Caribbean Mermaid was in a quiet street three blocks back from the sea front. There was a hairdressers next to the bar. It was one of the unusual features of Spanish centres of any size just how many hairdressers there were. He couldn't see how they could all pay their way but in his limited experience they all seemed to keep going somehow.

The bar he was sat in was a typical back street Spanish bar with a chalk board outside advertising a *menu del dia,* three courses for six euros with bread and a drink; incredible value for money. He had been told that it was some sort of legal requirement for *cafeterias* to provide this offer. There were all sorts of weird Spanish customs that Mack had come across. It added to the experience and helped him to realize that he was living in a foreign country, which sometimes it was easy to forget.

There was no-one on the terrace across the road and he could see a couple of bodies just inside the door. They were clearly there to monitor anyone coming in and decide if they were allowed in or not. As he sat there trying not to look as if he was taking any notice he spotted a large half shaven thug coming out of the door and heading off down the street. It didn't appear as if the bar had any paying customers at all, Mack wondered how it was supposed to make a living. He did wonder if it was supposed to make a living at all or if it was just a front. He would find out soon enough.

Mack left one euro fifty in coins on the table and left. You never paid in advance in Spain especially not in a Spanish bar. He knew that would be enough as all bars seemed to charge the same, between a euro and a euro twenty. Nobody had chased him down the road yet anyway.

Mack headed back to his car with his thinking cap on. He was unsure how to approach his introduction into the Ukrainian's lair. It would sort itself out one way or another thought Mack.

Heading out of Estepona Mack passed the Kempinsky Hotel, one of the leading hotels in the world and the destination for many a celebrity over the years. It wasn't a bad place to live thought Mack, he just needed to make it a bit less inviting for the bottom feeding scumbags that fed on misery and corruption. Well he was on with it.

CHAPTER 3

"Give us 50 pence"

It wasn't that Jack McLean was a psychopath with a vicious streak. It was just that you couldn't intimidate or bully him. If you tried, you regretted it, sooner or later. He didn't care if the arsehole trying to intimidate him thought he had got away with it at least temporarily. He was quite able to bide his time. He didn't simmer; he didn't get eaten away with anger. But you were gonna get it….big time.

When he was 11 years old he had entered rather a good school in Bradford. It didn't really matter whether the school was good or bad, they all had their share of bullies. Mack wasn't a big lad at the time and suffered the usual indoctrination that the other new boys had to as well. He was tied to a fence with his school tie and had mud splattered on his head. But this was the same for everybody and soon passed.

School life suited Mack. He had made a few school friends on top of the mates he hung around with at home. He was popular, he was bright and life was good. A few lads he knew had tried a cigarette round the back of the school. Mack wasn't interested; he couldn't see the point and he didn't feel the need to impress anyone. So Mack never touched a cigarette in his life.

The school contained a mixture of ethnicities as was common nowadays. Mack had no issue or opinion of anyone from whatever heritage. He hadn't been tainted at home by bias or prejudice and he judged as he found. It would be later in life that he formed his own views following his own experiences. For now he was happy to mix with anyone; it was a shame however that some of the ethnic minorities chose not to mix with anyone else. That was their loss.

One day a boy from the year above had collared him at lunchtime. "Oy! McLean, come here". The boy had a weasely look about him and wasn't a big specimen. He was, however, in a group of 3 similarly weasely ne'er-do-wells. "Give us 50 pence you little cunt". The boy had a sneering look and bad teeth. His uniform was worn and grubby and his shoes were dirty and had mismatched laces. His accomplices were equally ill kempt. This was an early example of like poles attracting; the mouthpiece with the two hangers-on. On their own the two lackeys would not have taken it upon themselves to seek out likely victims, they need leadership to follow and give them the means to be seen as part of a crew. Even at their young age they were forming a pattern of behaviour that would lead them directly down the path of crime. It was a straight road and, unless one or more of them was taken completely out of this cancerous environment the road would not deviate.

Young Mack was taken aback. He had never been confronted in this way. However a strange feeling came across him. If this wanker wanted his only 50 pence which was his bus fare, he was going to earn it. Outnumbered and cornered Mack did the thing that was going to make him anything but a soft target in future; he smashed the older boy in the nose. Before the other two could react he had grabbed the boy's hair and was hitting him as hard and as often as he could. "Gerroff me you little twat" wailed the boy. At this point the other two reacted and grabbed Mack holding him immobile with one arm each. The boy's nose was bleeding and he looked like he had been dragged through a privet. As much as Mack struggled he could not break free of the other boys' grip. "Right, you little cunt" said the older boy "you've fuckin' had it". With this he punched Mack in the face followed by another one to the stomach. Mack doubled up but refused to show pain. The boy then went into Mack's pocket and retrieved his only 50 pence. "I want this off you every week from now on" said the boy as he kicked him in the stomach and walked off with his henchmen. More than Mack's pride was hurt. His stomach was killing him and his lip was bleeding. He was sure of one thing however. He was not going to give that fucker another penny. He had gone to a good school because he was bright. Being bright helped him to understand that he couldn't match the boy physically, not with his fists anyway. Nor could he take on the boy with his cronies present. But he would take the boy on. That weekend he asked his dad to take him to the community centre where a karate school was holding enrolments. The classes were held on a Tuesday and Friday with weekends available for keener students who wanted to advance their skills. Mack would attend every minute available. It would take time unfortunately for Mack to develop both the skills and physical development to make a difference; especially taking on boys older and bigger than him. And he did have a more immediate problem with the Artful Dodger; a problem he intended to solve.

The following week he followed the bully boy from school and found out where he lived. Not surprisingly, a sink estate on the wrong side of town. The garden resembled a scrapyard and one of the upstairs windows was filled in with hardboard. The only shops had no windows; these had been boarded up deliberately with metal cages covering the outside. Typical of these areas, the locals would rob their local facility without consideration of the service it provided to the community as a whole. In fact the only consideration was their own selfish need for easy money to buy designer trainers and track suits, drugs and weapons. This was Mack's first real exposure to the environment he was to become all too familiar with. This was also the point when a philosophy was firmly fixed in Mack's young mind. Why, just because you were raised in a shithole, did you have the right (or believe you had the right) to intimidate other people either for violent ends or financial gain? Others may be intimidated but Mack wasn't wired that way.

Mack's dad was quite a good pool player and played for the local pub team. He owned a quality cue that split into two pieces. There was no way his dad would simply lend him the cue. It was made of ash with rosewood butt inlaid with veneers. Mack considered the idea of using it in retribution but the consequences were too severe to contemplate; any weapon would do even though he loved the feel of the pool cue butt. It had a lovely balance, not too heavy and not too light. You could swing it with devastating speed and it would not break. No, he couldn't use this but its suitability was something that stuck with him.

He concealed a suitable length of wood outside the school so he could pick it up later. After school Mack followed the boy and got on the same bus, taking a seat downstairs at the back. He got off at the stop before the boy's and jogged after the bus. Seeing the boy get off he followed him down a quiet back alley that smelled of piss and dog shit that led to his house. Mack called out to him "Oy fuckwit". As the boy turned he adopted his trademark sneer. "What are you doing you little cunt?" Mack didn't answer but pulled the wood from under his coat and held the thinner end. "What you gonna do with that" was what the tosser started to say, but this was to set the tone for every such encounter the Mack would engage in for the rest of his life. All the mongrel managed to say was "What you....." before Mack swung the club. He didn't however swing it in a roundhouse style where the bully could possibly parry or even catch it. No, he brought it straight down from behind his head and onto the shoulder blade of the boy. Mack seemed to have some natural ability or instinct to know how to inflict maximum damage or pain. This immediately rendered the boy in severe pain (remember, the boy was only 13 years old himself). Mack then swung the cue catching him on the side of the head. Mack was not yet big or strong enough to cause major damage but the effect was adequate. As the boy protected his head from further blows, Mack swung the stick into his forearm. At this point the boy started to panic and plead, something Mack would come across time and again from these lowlife scum. "Stop it! I think my arm is broken!" A look approaching fear was in the boy's eyes. This wasn't the time to stop however and Mack swung the cue once more across the boy's back. The boy was now in serious pain and starting to blub. "Please stop" he whimpered. Mack knew he had him at this point. "I am never going to give you the steam off my shit you cunt. If I even feel your presence I promise I will come looking for you and I will leave you in a bleeding heap in the gutter". At this Mack wiped the stick on the boy's coat and threw it over a garden wall. Mack fixed him with a strange stare "Never get brave or cocky and always remember this. I'll cripple you next time". After taking a quid from the boy's pocket, Mack walked off leaving the blubbering boy to slink off to his hovel where his mum cracked him round the head for getting blood on his shirt.

This encounter set Mack's mind firm. You didn't need to be bigger or stronger than shit bags who thought they could get one over on you. You did need to be determined however to realize that; no matter what the circumstances, they would never get the upper hand. Mack had a switch in his head. When it was off he was one of the guys, great company with a great sense of humour. When it flipped however he knew no boundaries. As he grew he learned to control his emotions and his martial arts training would help tremendously in terms of focus. But if somebody crossed his red line he could maintain his control to devastating effect. Never allowing the red mist to take over and render him out of control. It was just that the cunt in front of him lost any human attributes. They were less than animals (he was kind to animals), there was no going back - they would suffer.

CHAPTER 4

Jimmy Arduznales

Every town in the world had one. We usually came across them in our early teens. As you stretched your young wings, attending the youth club or going on the bus to hang around town in the coffee shops you got your first glimpse and your first warning. "That's Jimmy Arduznales (I made that name up to cover all such shitheads), don't even look at him he'll kill you". You caught a glimpse of a scruffy cunt who walked with an exaggerated shoulder swing - just a T shirt on no matter the weather. If you got close enough you would see the bad teeth and the bad skin, both the result of a diet of chips and full fat Coke. Not real Coca Cola you understand, no, the shit you bought in the discount store for 30p for a two litre bottle.

Jimmy Arduznales was always on the lookout for someone who was actually looking at him. This was his role in life, to ask them "what the fuck you looking at?" About 95% of the poor unfortunates he asked the question to would quickly look away mumbling "nothing mate, I don't want no bother". These were the ones he would then continue his verbal assault with. "Don't ever look at me you cunt, I'll fucking stab you in the eye. Fucking wanker." The mumbling soul would shuffle off grateful that he had survived his encounter with Jimmy Arduznales,

Then there was the other 5%. Most of these were brave enough to answer the question with "Don't know it hasn't got a label". This was enough to get Jimmy Arduznales to his feet. "Are you trying to be funny you cunt?" To which the brave idiot would reply "whoa! calm down, I was only having a laugh, don't make a big deal of it" slowly backing away. "Funny fucker aren't you? Fuck off before I smack that smile off your face". Authority established Jimmy Arduznales was briefly satisfied.

Then there were the few that were of a similar ilk to Jimmy Arduznales. They maybe knew him by reputation and were up for a challenge, or they were blissfully unaware that he was a psychopathic monster with blatant disregard as to how much punishment was enough.

You see, Jimmy Arduznales had to fight to survive. To survive his home environment such as it was. To survive his sink estate, to survive attending school, on the occasions that he did. In his mind the only way was to fight your way to the top. But fighting in the world he lived in was not squaring up to an opponent and swinging a few punches. No, everyone –absolutely everyone he would come across – carried a blade. Most encounters ended in a serious, or deadly, knife wound. It was survival, not of the fittest, but of the most evil vicious fucker on the estate or even on the few filthy streets that were your limited world. He could fight with his fists and feet and would have no problem kicking an opponent beyond unconsciousness. But he preferred to inflict damage and serious injury with whatever he could lay his hands on at the time; bricks, bottles, blades, glasses you name it he would use it.

So, on the occasion that someone answered the call "who you looking at you cunt?" they answered "I'm looking at you arsehole, what are you going to do about it?" Jimmy Arduznales would press launch control. Flying at his challenger instantaneously. No warning, no banter, no "come outside" just an explosion of absolute violence, head, fists, feet, beer glasses, bottles, anything. The challenger may be a local hard man himself but he had no answer to the assault that was coming his way; left in a bloody heap with some shocked onlooker calling an ambulance.

So then you got "that's Jimmy Arduznales, he just put Johnny Madboy in hospital, don't even look at him he's fucking mental as anything"

What you then have is reputation, respect, fear, status, in fact all the ingredients of a gang leader; someone who would command an entourage of hangers-on. Other lowlifes who thought they were 'hard' by association. These would become Jimmy Arduznales army. He could direct this army to do his bidding; enforcement of territory, distribution of drugs, robbery you name it. This is a world that exists beyond the scope of the average town dweller. People who worked hard for a living, raising families and having a pint down the local would have no concept of this undergrowth of evil doing. They would hear of a drive-by shooting in Tower Hamlets or Moss Side on the news or some black teenager who had been stabbed to death outside a newsagents in Wolverhampton. This would register for a few fleeting seconds before they carried on with the cryptic crossword, still looking for an answer to 24 across.

As you know, I made Jimmy Arduznales up. Complete fiction. But I am willing to wager a small amount that nearly all readers of this chapter recognize someone from their youth. In all towns in all the countries of the world there are people and situations like this. You could argue the nature/nurture debate; you could say that Jimmy Arduznales would not exist if he had a better home environment and/or education. But you could have a Jimmy Arduznales being expelled from Eton. And instead of going on to be a Cabinet Minister he would be the head of a high end embezzling organization. Bribing policemen and arranging the elimination of competition. Savile Row suit or track suit it matters not. Tokyo or Tamworth,

Jimmy Arduznales is alive and well and coming to your local pub sometime soon. Just don't look at him.

CHAPTER 5

"Ippon!"

Mack continued with his martial art studies. He was fortunate only because the club he had joined was not a "belt happy" club looking for brownie points through the amount of high colour belt holders it possessed. No, the Bradford Karate Centre was a fighting club that entered all the local and national tournaments and always came away with a hatful of trophies. The association was founded by Greg Skelton who had made his reputation in national contests as the best heavyweight in the country. He had then set up his own association with its own style, a factor in the proliferation of clubs and strange style names. You had Shotokan, Wadu Ryu, Renshinkai among many others There was money in martial arts and much of the mystique and heritage of the sport was diluted by any number of individuals promoting their style as the best, when in fact they had made it up as a variation on a theme. Notwithstanding this, the Sensei at the club was an enthusiastic tutor and insisted on discipline and attention to detail. He was also willing to take on outstanding students and give them the extra time and tuition.

All karate and tae kwon do clubs are the same no matter the style or the country. Hours and hours of marching up and down the *dojo* practicing punches, kicks and block and all the while counting to ten in Japanese. *Ichi, ni, san, shi, go, roku, shichi, hachi, ku, juu.* The last number often replaced with a loud shout or scream for added power. This shout varied from club to club, there was no right or wrong way as long as it wasn't too high pitched and sounded like a *kung fu* movie.

Marching up and down, up and down, *ichi, ni, san*....... Every punch or kick focussed on a particular point in space. Eyes staring at this imaginary point so that every blow landed in the same place then moving onto bag work usually in groups of about four students. Punching or kicking the bag in exactly the same place. *Ichi, ni, san*.....Then pairing up, with another student, one with had pads and the other with light mitts and foot pads. Punching and kicking in exactly the same place. Drilling that focus in so that every punch or kick could be directed with unerring accuracy.

Many would never enter competitions and would never dream of using their skills outside the *dojo*. They were there for the training and fitness and the martial arts would provide this to an extremely high degree. They may go for a pint of orange juice afterwards; they just enjoyed being a part of something that enhanced their daily lives.

In common with many clubs such as this there was a wide range of students in Mack's club ranging from five year old girls to seventy five year old pensioners. There wasn't really an age that was unsuitable for any of the martial arts. Whether it was karate, judo, jui jitsu or any of the many other styles you could study there were a few major aspects of the training. Firstly, fitness was key and then speed plus focus along with respect, self-discipline, meditation and dedication. For young people these factors were a real bonus to their personal development and, in a good club with good instructors, the martial arts, whether they were ever used in real life or not, provided life lessons as well as physical development.

Within this environment Mack thrived. Some clubs would push a student through to black belt in a couple of years. Mack's club believed you were ready when you were good enough. And you would not be good enough for at least 4 years. Attention to detail meant that when students of the BKC performed a *Kata* (a series of choreographed moves) it was precise and powerful. As you moved through the belts, the *katas* became more and more complicated. Black belt *katas* were typically over 100 moves each of which had to be perfectly executed. By the time he was 16 Mack was one of the outstanding juniors in the country. He had attained Sho dan, his first grade black belt. In competition, particularly in Kumite (one to one fighting) he was untouchable but because he was dedicated to improving his fighting style, his kata suffered and he struggled both in competition and in grading. To this end he decided to try another style. Tae Kwon Do was about to be introduced to the Olympics and karate wasn't. He decided to join a local club and see if there were aspects of the sport that could improve him. Etiquette dictated that he start at the lowest grade - white belt, but his existing skills and natural ability plus his obsessive dedication ensured his rapid rise through the ranks.

Tae Kwon Do is the Korean equivalent of karate and, apart from the language, the moves and techniques were similar. One of the key differences was that Tae Kwon Do used more protective gear and generally was more full contact (although technically wasn't supposed to be). Furthermore this particular club encouraged the breaking of boards with hand and foot. The boards were specially produced plastic panels that clipped together in the middle and broke in two with a blow or kick. About one and a half cm thick you could place one or more together to provide a harder target. If punching you would normally use a light mitt for protection but kicks were with the bare heel. What this did was focus the young McClean mind on strength of kick or punch with accuracy being paramount. Eventually he could power through five boards with a punch and seven boards with a spinning back roundhouse kick. No-one could do this in his club; his power and focus were incredible.

Martial arts are supposed to teach control of mind and body but inevitably certain individuals would take up a style and join a club with the intention of using the techniques outside the *Dojo*. They would use punches and kicks to inflict damage on members of the public that could not defend themselves as a trained athlete would. This was generally unacceptable but these idiots were not in it for the sport or personal development. They enjoyed the fact that they had been taught how to punch or kick an opponent to severely injure them. The problem with these arseholes however was that; their targets weren't opponents, they were victims.

Now, anyone with a basic understanding of martial arts will know that, what goes on on a mat does not necessarily transfer to the street. The other problem is that these potential thugs would not obey the rules of semi-contact when training in the *Dojo*. Henceforth many a broken nose or dislocated finger or wrist was suffered by their unwitting sparring partners. Mack's intolerance of bullies meant that he was going to have to sort one or more of these dickheads out sooner rather than later.

Mack gained his black belt in Tae Kwon Do in an incredible 18 months. Tae Kwon Do was never going to satisfy his desire for improvement however. He couldn't see a progression in a discipline he didn't really have a connection with. Karate was his sport of choice and, having achieved his goal, he returned to The Bradford Karate Club. Aged 18 and now showing the physical maturity that was to give him such an advantage in speed and power Mack dedicated himself and graded to second Dan.

During a competition at the Woolwich Arsenal Sports Centre in London, Mack was matched to a shaven headed opponent in the 75 kilo plus *Kumite*. Mack had watched his opponent previously and was aware that A. he was good and B. he was overly aggressive. As Mack progressed through the rounds of the competition with relative ease and he knew this would be the round he would need to get through to reach the semi-final.

Competition *Kumite* is scored a half point (*waza ari*) or one full point (*ippon*) at a time within a two minute contest and the fight is stopped at each point or half point after scoring punch or kick is registered. As the fight started the thug managed to get a kick through Mack's guard and landed in his stomach. This scored *waza-ari* - half a point. First to two points wins. On the restart Mack feinted a punch to draw his opponent's guard and followed up with a perfectly executed *mawashi geri* (roundhouse kick) to the head. The kick was landed with minimum force but contacted and scored *ippon*(full point). The *karateka* started again and the skinhead was clearly not happy. Even though his opponent was wearing a gumshield, Mack could see he was mad as a March hare. Even though Mack was ready for the action, he was not ready for the ferocity in which the attack was delivered. There is a big difference between semi-contact and full-contact. And there is a world of difference between full-contact and outright full-on assault. Good as he was, Mack was not prepared for this and the thug delivered two or three full on punches to Mack's face followed by a *mae geri* (front driving kick) to the solar plexus that sat Mack firmly on his arse. Not satisfied with this, the thug then went to deliver an axe kick to Mack's chest that would have broken his ribs. Fortunately, Mack was still too quick for this and rolled out of the way. Now we had a problem. The thug was warned by the match referee for excessive use of force and Mack was given a moment to recover. After a few seconds the combatants faced each other again and Mack knew immediately that there was more to come. Little did the twat know, but he had just made a big mistake. Stepping across his front foot Mack delivered a spinning roundhouse kick of such force that, even though Bully Boy tried to parry it, it went straight through his guard and in to his floating rib. He was immediately winded and sank to his knees Mack followed up with a straight kick to the side temple that sparked the idiot out. He turned and bowed to the judge and walked off the mat knowing full well that he was disqualified. Mack didn't enter any more competitions.

CHAPTER 6

"Come outside"

Aged 19 Mack graded to Third Dan which was the highest grade you could achieve through ability alone. Further Dan grades were subsequently awarded by the association you were a member of as a reward for your contribution to the cause, either by running a club or being involved in the running of a region or area. Many people think that 7th Dan holders are super masters of a martial art. Often this is far from the case as, usually, they gave up full-on intensive training years ago. They are simply further up the ladder of achievement not necessarily of ability. Having achieved what Mack believed to be the pinnacle of his sport Mack chose to leave his club as the outside influences of work and women were occupying too much of his time. It was also around this time that Mack started to use the local gym to develop his physical strength. As mentioned earlier. Mack did not want to build size but wanted to be strong as well as mobile, fast and effective. He was all of these. He had a six pack like a wash board (for those of you who can remember what a wash board looks like), his shoulders were wide and powerful and his biceps and triceps were developed to fine definition. He still practiced his kicks and punches plus he maintained an incredible flexibility that allowed him to place a kick on the temple of some 6'6" dickhead if he needed to.

Saturday nights were spent in the bars around town. Usually a pub-crawl around the popular night spots. He liked particularly the 'Victory Lounge' a traditional Victorian pub that retained much of its old world charm. Plus, the juke box had a great selection of classic Northern Soul Hits. Slotting in a pound coin Mack selected Jerry Butler's rendition of 'Moody Woman' a real dance track.

Mack was a good looking guy, tall and toned and he didn't have too much trouble attracting the ladies. Inevitably in these situations some local ne'er do well would think that he had more of a calling with a certain young lady than Mack did. You know the type, not good looking and a seriously bad attitude but, by some miracle, they had had a couple of dates with a real looker and thought that the unfortunate girl should not enjoy the company of anyone else – ever.

So it was that Mack was dancing away with an attractive young lady on the dance floor of the "Coliseum" night club when a stocky shaven headed arsehole with a tattoo of a swallow on his neck appeared in front of him. "Who do you think you are fuckface, Casanova?" asked the foul breathed individual. "Just chancing my arm" replied Mack with no threat in his voice. "Yeah well I'm going out with her so leave the fuck alone alright?" he said. Mack simply shrugged and said "I've been watching her all night and she is not with anybody as far as I can see". The sneering arsewipe got right into Mack's face giving him the full force of his halitosis. "She thinks she's finished with me but I'm telling you otherwise so back the fuck off or I'll knock yer the fuck out!". The thugs eyes were wide with threat, his top lip drawn back and his shoulders were doing a strange side to side thing whilst his head kept still and staring. Apparently this would have intimidated most average clubbers and Mack took note of the lanky streak of shit that was manoeuvring himself behind his mate. "Why don't you get on with it then?" opening his arms wide with palms turned up by way of invitation. The reply non-plussed the dickhead who said "I'm not doing you in here so gerroutside you cunt" Going 'outside' had long ceased to be an option for Mack. What was 'going outside' going to achieve? Were Queensberry rules to be applied? Would they have time to take their jackets off and hand them to their 'seconds'? Maybe have a little warm up? Why let the fuckers be prepared or organise help when you were not going to be allowed back in the club anyway? As the cocky twat turned to take Mack outside he did not see the side kick that smashed into the back of his neck. Instantly recovering his stance Mack drove a punch straight into the bridge of the lanky git's nose ending his involvement (the bean-pole swore later that Mack had used a pool cue). The stocky one did not go down as the kick had simply propelled him forward and he turned with fists clenched ready to do battle. Mack allowed him to take a swing before deftly side stepping the punch and delivering a withering blow to the side temple. This stunned the idiot but not as much as the round house kick that landed square on his nose. Give him his due, the skinhead was game for a go and Mack realized that this was not your ordinary opponent. Frequently clubbers would be high on drink and cocaine and did not feel the blows - as hard as they may be. Knowing he would have to take the wanker out, Mack delivered a straight punch to the solar plexus. This took the wind out of his sails and Mack proceeded to pummel the living daylights out of the bloke. Hammer blow after hammer blow rained into the thugs face until the security staff decided to step in and try to separate the two. Stocky bloke was still not unconscious such was the level of recreational drugs in his system; however he was simply a bloody mess. This taught Mack a lesson in assessing potential opponents; he realized he would have to almost kill one of these fuckers sooner or later. So be it.

CHAPTER 7

Sorting the problem

Mack needed to avoid digging a hole. He had taken on a task which involved dealing with nasty evil fuckers on each side of the equation; working for a bald drug dealing thug in Puerto Banus, and looking to make contact with a bunch of evil Ukrainian drug dealing thugs in Estepona. Decisions had to be made and Mack could make decisions when required. The back door approach would probably not work and would take too long. These wankers were so paranoid you could not go in and observe without being noticed and threatened so it would have to be the front door or walk away and look a twat. Front door it was. Mack made a call to Handforth in Puerto Banus. "Handy man! Listen I need a small favour, I need the name of the Big Knob round here so I can ask for him in person?" Handforth was confused, "how come you're asking me for something you should know already?" Mack needed the info without looking as if he was clueless. "This isn't as straight forward as it looked. These ruskies are a close knit bunch and I would rather not make more enemies than I need to by beating the shit out of half of them". "OK , look, you need to find a bloke called Vlad. Yeah, I know, it's a stupid name but you know what these rusky gangsters are like; they want to sound like Putin. Anyway he's the man around there and I don't think he invites Brits for tea very often".

By the way, we all know that Ukrainians are not Russian and vice-versa but Lee Handforth didn't pass geography; how could he, he didn't go to school. Mack could hear the challenge and slight humour in Handforth's tone. "Yeah, I'd sort of worked that one out. I've got a bit of a plan so stand by your bed". Mack ended the call and headed for the centre of Estepona looking for the Caribbean Mermaid.

Now, here's the rub. Mack was working for Lee Handforth (full description as previously) and needed to sort some form of communication with a Ukrainian idiot who called himself Vlad. The object of the operation was to smooth the import, sale and distribution of some 5 kilos of grade A heroin. Or so the thugs thought. Mack's intention was that none of this evil substance would make it to the streets. He had seen first-hand the impact that this awful drug had on individual lives. Heroin abuse led to lives of crime or prostitution or both. Totally addictive after only a few doses the drug had such a grip on the body that the addict would go to any lengths to obtain the next fix.

Based on opium it had usually started life in the fields of Afghanistan or some other Asian country. The pure resin was processed from the seeds of the opium poppy and then transported in its pure form to various destinations throughout the world. As a plant based substance it basically cost almost nothing to produce so; even though it was worth millions as an end product, it mattered not if a few shipments got intercepted – there was plenty more where that came from.

So it was the sheer volume of product being constantly shipped the ensured that enough got through to supply the desperate end user. British Asians were importing foodstuffs, silk, ornaments and myriad other products in huge volumes. Their methods of concealment had been honed over decades and the Border Forces of the various destinations were simply putting their finger in the dyke; they couldn't stem the flood. Once arrived at its destination it travelled through the supply chain, at each stage being 'cut' with other chemicals till eventually arriving at the street with about 15% potency. This was fine for the addict. It had to be diluted to be tolerated in the quantities taken. This was how someone could be a heroin addict for years. So long as the products used to 'cut' the heroin were of sufficient quality the body could survive years of addiction.

This was fine as long as you could afford decent heroin from a decent dealer. However, when the money ran out the cravings didn't. And heroin withdrawal was tortuous. Severe cramps, cold sweats, uncontrolled shaking and an emptiness that cannot be described to the uninitiated. This drove an addict to go to any lengths to obtain their next 'fix'. Usually starting with emptying their own bank account, then the bank account of any other unsuspecting person, then selling anything of value and finally to rock bottom. Break-ins, shop-lifting, mugging, prostitution (male and female), begging; in fact anything, absolutely anything to get another fix.

Heroin addiction could take a law abiding, hard-working, property owning, car owning upstanding citizen to emaciated, filthy outcast in six months to a year.

To say that the purveyors of this misery could care less would be an understatement. You see, the purveyors of this misery didn't just supply the drug. They would lend the victim the money for their fixes and, inevitably, when the debt could not be re-payed, they would beat them, confiscate anything of value and ultimately sell their bodies to anyone desperate enough for a cheap shag.

A couple of years earlier Mack had come to the attention of the criminal classes when he took out two drug dealers while attending a Northern Soul club in Bradford. He knew full well that many clubbers took recreational drugs, legal highs and illegal uppers. This he tolerated as he enjoyed the scene so much even though he didn't need the extra help himself. In general, taking a bit of 'whizz' (amphetamine sulphate powder) now and again would not lead to further abuse and rarely to any adverse side effects.

The line was crossed with these two arseholes when Mack found out on the grapevine that they were dealing heroin to 18 year olds. Again greed comes into play. Not satisfied with making a few quid from selling a bit of powder and a few E's they had been encouraged by their supplier to expand the operation.

In this case Mack didn't wait for them to go outside or catch them up a dark alley. He simply walked up to them and smashed the living daylights out of the pair of them. I mean smashed.

Needless to say, word got back to the upper echelons of low-life land and 3 more thugs turned up at the next event. Mack knew the look. It was a look that stood out like a sore thumb among the smartly dressed and dedicated fashionistas of the Northern Soul circuit. Nobody would dare have a baseball cap on never mind backwards. Mack didn't need the hassle and simply walked up to the three and said "if you are here to see me I'll save you the trouble. Either fuck off or get the same treatment." In a group of three there is always a gobshite. This one was a cocky, skinny scruffy twat with the backwards baseball cap, the bad teeth (the NHS had a lot to answer for with the state of the nation's teeth), bum fluff on his chin "Are you the geezer who smacked our boys?" His demeanour was not conducive to a pleasant atmosphere. "Look cunt, you are in the wrong fucking place to come and have a go so what the fuck are you here for?" Mack had realised that the idiots must know that they were on a sticky wicket. His manner had the wankers raising their hands in a defensive gesture. ""Whoa! Whatevah, we've come to see if you will see our gaffer?" "What the fuck for?" asked Mack. "He wants to make a little arrangement wiv yer". This intrigued Mack. He would have expected a team to come and (try to) sort him out. He didn't expect a business meeting being proposed. He quickly realised that these people wanted a clear playing field in which to operate and wanted his compliance. They could have resorted to strong arm tactics put probably realised he was not your average Joe and that he was better off on the books. He also realised in an instant that he could potentially build a picture of activity that could be of some use.

"OK, only where I can see what's going on". Mack was curious and willing to take the next step to suss out how these low-life shitbags wanted to play it. "Yeah yeah, tomorrow morning 10 o'clock City Square". They turned and marched out, job done.

Mack wanted to know more about the makeup of this operation. Beating up a couple of low life street sellers wouldn't impact their operation although the state of their appearance after the 'Mack' treatment also made them realise that they could either try to sort the Mack problem out or see if it could be made easier. Also, quality violence such as Mack provided could be useful; this was the typical attitude of these gangster types.

Mack strolled into City Square at five to ten. City Square in Bradford was a wide open space next to the Victorian Town Hall and had been upgraded in recent years with a state-of-the-art fountain display with computer control. Dancing columns of water and, at night, a colourful lighting display provided a welcoming place for office workers to eat packed lunches with their headphones on and feed the pigeons. During warm summer days kids would splash around the shallow pool screaming with delight.

He had been there half an hour earlier to observe any untoward movements, potential traps and also exit routes. So far so good, these idiots probably thought they were untouchable anyway. Stood by the fountain were a couple of seedy looking characters with hoodies under 'Puffa' jackets, high value trainers and jeans that would look better on an orangutan. It's strange how these wankers were against any form of authority especially people in uniform and yet here they were in as much a uniform as was needed to easily identify them as criminals. Maybe that's slightly unfair but nevertheless it was easy for Mack to recognise who he was here to meet. Mack didn't break stride as he walked straight up to them and stood uncomfortably close without saying a word. There were three of the scum and, as always, only one mouthpiece. This particular piece if shit only needed a blue tooth for a snooker set. He had grey skin bordering on parchment over a skeletal face that indicated years of substance abuse. Under the hoodie his head was shaven and the overall look was of a skeleton peeking out from a shroud as in the image of Death most people would picture. His accomplices were no better in physical condition and Mack assumed it was simply their lack of any kind of moral fibre and their willingness to inflict harm in any way possible that had allowed them to move up any kind of social ladder; even though their ladder was extremely short. "So, you're the geezer that sorted my boys out?" Not so much as a "good morning". Mack held the tosser's gaze. "I simply made a point that you don't peddle your filth on my manor". The thug sneered "I could have you stuck like a pig you cunt, who do you think you are?" Mack's face showed no emotion "Now, I know why you wanted to meet here; it's not for my protection, it's for yours. Right now you had better say your piece and fuck off before I risk pasting your scabby face all over this square on CCTV" The drug peddling skeleton smiled although it was more of a rictus grin. He felt the violence emanating from Mack and he was well away from the security of the sink estate he festered in. "Look, I have a business to run, I have some interests in the Buttershaw estate and I can sort you out a few quid if you don't try to kill my boys every time they have a delivery" He pulled an envelope out of his Puffa jacket. "Here's a grand on account. That can be more if you want to come and work for me?" Mack took the envelope and then handed it straight back. "You can pay me when I've done something and I'll decide when that is, not you. So, what does working for you mean?" The thug seemed to relax a peg "I need somebody to run protection for my boys. Most of them are only kids and they work better if they know they are being looked after." At this point Mack had what he wanted. This arsehole thought that Mack was the answer to his problems, that money could remove all obstacles, that you could buy your way out of trouble. His unprovoked violence had given him a route into a bed of evil and he intended to put them out of business. He also had a direct line to the head of the snake. He also knew the authorities had their hands tied in investigating these outfits. They were bound by the law and procedure. Mack wasn't and he had an intense hatred towards scum who peddled misery for a living. Bullies, drug dealers, thieves and muggers. They all preyed on potentially good people. People who had been in the wrong place or with the wrong person or at the wrong time and who became entrapped in a life of addiction which, in turn, led to a life of crime and petty theft. Mack could make a difference in his own small way, and, however small, it would make Mack feel better. It wouldn't be now however, he had a good job and a clean slate. He wanted to keep it that way until he decided it was time to act.

CHAPTER 8

Working it out

On leaving school Mack had gone to work at a motor dealers in the parts department. A Vauxhall dealer, Mack got to know all about Astras, Insignias and Corsas. Not the best of jobs, but Mack wasn't cut out for college or university. The regular income was handy, such as it was but Mack quickly got bored. He was bright enough, very bright, but his talents were not necessarily academic. He had insight, he could read people. He was observant; he could weigh up situations quickly and react instantly. He was outwardly friendly, everyone liked Mack however those who got close to him knew there was a deep burning fire that could erupt when circumstances dictated. He never courted trouble or attention, he kept his own counsel. Around the local pubs and bars he was untroubled. The regulars about town had heard of or witnessed the odd occasion when Mack got upset. Sensible people kept on his right side.

Fortunately for Mack, and not a moment too soon he had been noticed by the sales manager. He could see that Mack was confident with a natural ability to talk to people and would be better suited in the sales department so he invited him to join the sales team and learn the ropes. This was right up Mack's street, he was born to sell. He always wore quality suits to work with expensive leather shoes. Tall, good looking, confident and with the gift of the gab he soon started earning good money and better still, he had the use of a company car. The latest model of Astra, a turbodiesel, shiny and new he loved driving around town showing off. It had a CD/MP3 player as well as a Bluetooth connection so he could play his favourite music with the window down. The girls loved it too. On more than one occasion he had to clean the seats after another conquest. Aged 20 he was earning enough to take his two week annual holiday in destinations further afield; Thailand, west coast USA, Sri Lanka. He was becoming more mature and worldly wise.

However, good fortune brings envy. Young men look at people like Mack and seethe with jealousy. When Mack took the car out he never drank alcohol. He could take it or leave it anyway.

One Saturday he had gone to a town centre bar to meet with a couple of mates and parked the car nearby. He left about 10 pm because he wanted to go home to watch Match of the Day. As he turned the corner to his car he saw three lads just walking away. Curious, he quickened his stride and as he reached his car he saw it had been 'keyed' down the side.

Now, we have established that Mack took up martial arts at the age of 11 and achieved black belt third Dan at Karate plus a black belt in Tae Kwon Do. We have also mentioned that disciplined fighting styles and techniques do not necessarily transfer outside the dojo. Ultimately there is no defence for a pool cue round the back of the head or a glass in the face if you are not expecting it. However, a high standard of martial arts does give you a couple of advantages (more than a couple actually). Strength, fitness, accuracy, power, flexibility, focus, patience to name but a few. Mack had all these in spades. More than these he had the burning fire deep down that would not allow him to back down or fail to act in the face of wrong doing. He also knew instinctively that to hesitate to act was often a fatal error. He knew that to strike first and hard gave a strategic advantage that was difficult to counter. In this instance the three low-lifes had not seen Mack come round the corner and were laughing their tits off twenty metres up the road. They were amused at the fact that Mack would come back to his shiny new car and find it badly scratched. Oh how he would be upset. "Ha ha fuck him" they gloated.

Mack didn't shout, he set off at a quick march and had closed the gap in a few seconds. The hindmost idiot was grabbed by the hair as Mack chopped him in the throat rendering him out of action choking and gagging. The other two spun round although neither quickly enough. One was despatched with a spinning roundhouse kick to the head and the other was about to pull something out of his pocket (good job he never got it out if it was a knife. That would have been a bigger mistake) Mack hit him on the bridge of his nose with a straight punch that dazed him and floored him with a withering blow right on the end of the chin. So, we have idiot one clutching his throat. Mack kicked him in his face and stamped on his nose leaving him unconscious and not pretty. Idiot two had been knocked out instantly with the kick. Mack rifled his pockets and found a bunch of keys. He used a Yale type key to rip the thug's nose open then threw the keys as far as he could. Thug three had a broken nose already. Mack gave him a broken cheekbone as well. Such was the way Mack dealt with these people. It was unlikely they would key anyone else's car and was guaranteed they would avoid him like the plague in future.

At work the next day Mack had to apologise to the sales manager for the state of his car. Fortunately the manager knew that it was not Mack's fault and he was also very fond of Mack so the car was booked in the paint shop and nothing more was said. The three wankers went to casualty with a tale of having been set upon by a rival gang. No, they didn't see them, couldn't remember anything; move on - lesson learned. So, age 20, Mack had a reputation. He wasn't so much feared as respected and that suited him. He didn't want to be seen in the same light as the lower classes but he didn't want to be a target for every drunken fool in town.

CHAPTER 9

Costa del Crime

The Costa del Sol (coast of the sun) ran from Algeciras, the most southerly point of mainland Spain, to Nerja before entering Granada province and changing to the Costa Tropical.

It was cheekily called the Costa del Crime due to the propensity for low life scum who were either on the run or too hot for comfort, to move there. Once there they could happily mingle with like-minded shitheads in darkened corners of tired bars planning how to earn an income from illicit means. They had never worked for a living in the legal, decent sense and weren't about to start now. Depending on how far up the ladder they had been in the UK dictated to some extent whether they would be a leader, committee member or lackey on the coast.

Quite often they came to an established patch of misery through a contact who had already made the move. Thus it became a conveyor belt of shit-bags moving into a business they were familiar with. It was as much a head hunting situation as in legitimate employment. In proper jobs you needed a CV and a good track record, possibly a recommendation. In shitbag land it worked the same. They were looking for someone with no moral fibre who would follow orders, give someone a good seeing to and come back to the bar for a beer. So they would put in a call to an old henchman and offer him a bit of sunshine. Which horrible motherfucker could refuse such an offer?

The gang leaders were the ones dishing out the orders and instructions, sat in a bar in a seedy corner of a coastal resort meant they were far from the sharp end when it came to Police intervention. These nasty fuckers had usually run out of options in the UK or whichever sink of Bohemian depravity they had crawled out from. Ukraine, Germany, Russia they all seemed to find a way to survive on the coast.

In Spain there are three main levels of police. The *Policia Local* who carried out general duties such as crossing control, parking misdemeanours and local licencing control of shops, bars etc.
The *Policia Nacional* were both uniformed and plain clothed. They were more like the UK CID looking for criminal activity wherever it may lurk. The good thing for the Brits and others on the coast was that they had enough on their plate with Spanish or Moroccan illegal activity that they spent only small efforts on other foreigners.
The *Guardia Civil* were the green uniformed, jack

booted remnant of General Franco's regime. The first thing they had to go through upon induction was a complete personality bypass. They policed the roads and motorways, setting up roadblocks randomly and searching people and vehicles for no reason whatsoever. They ran drug enforcement and were generally feared and grudgingly respected throughout the land.

Many non-Spaniards don't understand or consider how relatively recent was the fascist regime of General Francisco Franco Bahamonde who was a Spanish general who led the Nationalist forces in overthrowing the Second Spanish Republic during the Spanish Civil War. From 1939 until his death in 1975 he ruled with an iron fist and was responsible for some 30,000 to 50,000 deaths through forced labour, concentration camps and executions. Even following his death Spain was seriously behind in social and industrial development. Before 1976 you could buy no other vehicle but a SEAT and they were nothing like the modern VW based product of today. Only in the 1990's following Spain's acceptance into the European Union did significant infrastructure developments take place.

One of the legacies of Franco's reign is that, generally, the Spanish do as they are told. No one would have thought that they would give up smoking in bars but they did, instantly. The other legacy was that, if the Guardia Civil stopped you for any reason, you didn't get cocky.

So going under the radar of the *Policia Nacional* or the *Guardia Civil* was paramount for the criminal fraternity. However, because they had little or no knowledge of police activities in Spain, they underestimated them at their peril. Once "on the radar" the Spanish services, on land and at sea, had all the nous, resources and equipment to collar even the cleverest of criminal scum. And when you got your collar felt by the Spanish authorities you didn't consider taking them on and possibly escaping. These weren't your polite British Bobbies. They all carried guns and they had a mean streak. They would gladly beat the shit out of anyone resisting arrest without fear of anyone claiming unnecessary force. In Spain they didn't know the meaning.

The popular resorts on the coast were Torremolinos, Benalmadena, Fuengirola, Marbella and Estepona. There were smaller conurbations such as La Cala de Mijas, Calahonda and Elviria among others. The UK government reckoned there were some 500,000 ex-pat brits living on the coast but these were only the ones that registered as foreigners and generally contributed to the Spanish economy in some way or other. However there were probably almost as many more who were unregistered. They didn't drive legally registered cars, they paid their rent in cash or bunked with others who were equally undetectable. They drank in bars with like-minded scum in dingy corners, placing bets with illegal bookies, watching illegally streamed UK sports and dealing in illegal substances to one extent or another. Somehow they managed to survive at least a season or two.

This aspect of life on the coast rarely affected the general tourist industry. The golfers and tourists stayed in decent hotels or stayed in pre-booked apartments. They ate and drank in the better bars and restaurants. Argentinian steakhouses, Spanish Gastrobars, glass fronted tapas bars with white leather sofas on the terrace. You wouldn't find the scumbags there; unless you went to Puerto Banus where the likes of Lee Handforth lurked. But more of that later.

So the Costa del Sol was a game of two halves. Its main industry was providing quality leisure facilities and accommodation to tourist from the whole of Europe and beyond plus golf facilities during the winter months for born-again fifty something year old teenagers.

Beneath this was a rotten underworld of drug dealing and prostitution. Human trafficking from North Africa, processing of high-end vehicle thefts going from north to south and across to Africa. Ultimately you paid your money and made your choice. A nice holiday or golf tour or a subsistence level existence as long as you could stand it in some stinking flat.

CHAPTER 10

Dojang (training facility for tae kwon do)

There are over 50 golf courses on the Costa del Sol and Mack had considered having a go but thought it may be too much of a distraction. His main focus was maintaining his fitness and sharpness and to this end there were no shortage of gyms and fitness facilities on the coast. He needed however, to keep up with his martial arts training. Because his Spanish speaking was average at best he was reluctant to attend a Spanish *dojo*.

By fortune, one day he was having a quiet bottle of Mahou in his local bar the "Paradise" bar in Fuengirola. The Paradise was one of the bars popular with ex-pat residents and was owned by a former rugby league professional from Halifax, Yorkshire. It had an eight ball pool table in the entrance and a pavement terrace with a few chairs and tables set up with large umbrellas for shade. Mack preferred to sit at the bar where you got to join in with various conversations with other bar flies. The walls were lined with mirrors giving a feeling of space and the bar was covered in traditional Spanish tiles as were so many other bars.

I don't know what it is about bars that are open all day but there was always some idiot who thought that drinking twelve hours a day was a good idea. We also know that there are good drunks and bad drunks. Generally they are all a nuisance in some shape or form if you are completely sober. So it was that Mack was sitting quietly nursing a sparkling water (he generally didn't take alcohol during the day) when a bloke came up to him for no reason and offered his hand to shake. Not wanting to be rude Mack shook the man's hand and then immediately regretted it, realizing the idiot was already steaming at 3PM. "Alright pal?" said the drunk. ""I'm fine thanks" said Mack trying not to make eye contact. "Top man" said the drunk offering his hand once again.

What is it about drunks when they want to shake your hand all the time? Fucking annoying. At this point Mack had already learned that if you give these tossers an inch they would stick to you like glue talking shite and generally ruining your day. "Listen pal, do us a favour and fuck off will you?" Mack knew that you simply could not engage these people with any kind of pleasantries. "What the fuck" said the drunk "what have I done. I'm only trying to be polite, fuck me you're a charmer aren't you?" This could now go one of two ways and Mack didn't care which it was. The drunk would either wander off and bother somebody else or he get a bit lairy and ask Mack who he thought he was. Fortunately, in this case, the drunk shuffled off mumbling under his breath. Mack didn't give a fuck what he was saying as long as he went away. Another chap sat at the bar made eye contact with Mack and gave him a knowing smile. "Hard work aren't they?" asked the man. "Yeah" said Mack, "I'm just glad he didn't get revved up, I don't need it at this hour". "I know what you mean" said the man who then got up and moved towards Mack holding out his hand. "Martin" he said. Mack could see he had a bottle of non-alcoholic beer in his hand. "Jack McClean, most people call me Mack" he said taking the man's hand.

"On holiday?" asked Mack. "No, live here" replied the chap in a clearly northern UK accent. People from other parts of the UK or other English speaking countries would be amazed at how little needed to be said by northern English folk to be considered a conversation.

"Retired?" asked Mack. He had been on the coast long enough by now to know that you never asked anyone what they did simply because you rarely got a straight answer. The stock reply to the question "what do you do then" was "a bit of this, a bit of that". It was the strangest thing that, even if it was legal, most people did not like discussing how they earned or scraped a living. This was mostly because there were no proper or decent jobs to be had on the coast. There was also this strange mind-set where expat residents of the coast were so determined not to have to go back to the UK they would do absolutely anything to earn a crust. So you would have an engineer washing up in a local restaurant or a nurse cleaning apartments. For some reason, ex-pats were obsessed with the abundant sunshine. They believed that; as long as they were in the sun they were happy, although, more than often, they were skint and living hand to mouth.

"Not just yet, got a few years to go." replied the chap. "I actually teach Tae Kwon Do in the local church hall. I also sell a few DVD's to local people, better quality than the 'looky looky' men."*

All of a sudden Mack sat up in a much more interested kind of way. "Really? When do you have classes?" "Oh, are you interested?" asked the man. "I most certainly am" said Mack perking up noticeably.

"We meet on Tuesdays and Fridays at St Catherine's English church in Los Boliches, have you done any before? You look in good shape"
"Actually I have a dan grade, and I should point out I am also 3rd dan at karate but I am looking for somewhere to train" "wow!" said Martin. "We might be a bit below your level!" "No chance" said Mack. "I am happy to help out with training in classes as long as I can have at least some time to run through some personal routines"

"Well I'm sure you will be able to show us all a thing or two!" said Martin "come along on Tuesday at seven and I'll introduce you to the rest of the group. I only ask for 5 euros to help pay for the hall. I would normally say that grading is extra but I don't think you will be doing much of that!" "Great! said Mack I'll be looking forward to it".

* For the record a 'looky looky' man is a street seller from Senegal selling copy watches and sunglasses and known as such because of the request to tourists to 'looky looky' which they hadn't done for years but the name had stuck.

CHAPTER 11

"You don't like me do you?"

Mack turned up on the Tuesday evening at the church hall. It wasn't so much as a church hall as a large room below a block of apartments. There was no church as such, the 'church hall' was the church and the hall and the meeting room and anything else it needed to be. The main thing though was that it served the ex-pat community with a Protestant facility among the overtly Catholic Spanish. Martin introduced him to the rest of the group without really giving away his martial arts background.

Clearly when they got changed and Mack tied up his black belt they had a clue. It is a general courtesy in martial art circles to respect a belt grade even if gained through another association or club. Martial arts warm ups are a mixture of stretches, routine press-ups, sit-ups, star jumps and then repetitive punches and kicks whilst counting to ten in either Japanese or Korean according to the style you were practicing.

During this it was clear to the other trainees that Mack took his training extremely seriously. His practice punches and kicks were delivered with precision and power. Martin appreciated this as it would give the class a boost in effort automatically, something to aspire to.

After warm up Martin asked Mack if he would take some juniors through their basic 'forms'. These are the same as 'katas' in karate, a set of preset moves simulating a fight against an imaginary opponent. "OK" said Mack "who can tell me the name of the first form?". One girl of about twelve put up her hand. "What's your name?" asked Mack. "Amy" replied the girl. "OK, what's the name of the first form Amy?" "Il Jang" replied the girl. "Well done" said Mack. "Now, can you show me the first move?" Martin had clearly gone through the basics well. The first thing was to adopt the 'joonbi' ready stance with feet shoulder width apart and hands forming a fist facing inwards at waist level. "Very good" said Mack, "now show me the first move of the form". Amy turned to the side and performed a low block. "OK" said Mack, "that was pretty good but do you know what the form is actually for?" "To practice your moves?" suggested Amy. "Well, you will be practicing your moves in the form, but it is actually to represent a fight against one or more opponents". The group looked interested. "This is why, when performing the form, each move should be precise, powerful and show awareness that there is an opponent in front of you. In fact, if you think this way you will improve your forms all the way through your belts. So with this in mind the first move is actually to look to your left before moving, and then to block the kick that you now see coming, OK?" Mack took up the joonbi stance and showed the group with power and precision how the move should be carried out. "So remember, every time you turn you are looking at a different opponent and either kicking, punching or blocking that opponent. So look first and put real effort into your moves. And one more thing, when you shout during a move to generate power, make it count. During a real contest or fight this can give you a real advantage."

Mack then watched the group take this advice on board giving tips here and there, adjusting stances and encouraging effort.

After a while the class got together for group instruction from Martin and then they put on their protective mitts and foot-guards, helmets and chest protectors to practice sparring. This was the part Mack had always liked best, mainly because he was so good at it. He had a natural balance and evasiveness that made him extremely difficult to pin down and make contact with. He could read an opponent's intention so well he was on the move before the strike got anywhere near him. After a few of the class had tried their luck with similar standard classmates Martin said to Mack "come on then, let me see what I am up against!" Tae kwon do is semi-contact bordering on full-contact with due respect to members of the same dojang. Martin was a qualified instructor and second grade black belt and was no mug on the mat. Mack blocked a couple of nifty kicks and punches landing a couple of well timed scoring blows himself. However Martin's downfall was getting too cocky and trying to power through with a front kick. Mack easily blocked the kick, grabbed his collar and swept him to the mat following up with a driving downward punch and scream that stopped half an inch from his nose. Mack stood up and offered his hand to his instructor then bowing after pulling him upright.

"I'm glad you are on my side!" said Martin. "Just as a matter of interest are you interested in competitions with other associations?" Mack gave him a soft smile and just said "no".

In the Paradise bar there was a six foot four scumbag called 'Big Phil'. Big Phil took cocaine and drank - a lot. He fancied himself as something of a local gangster and drug dealer. He didn't deal drugs in the Paradise bar but he made a nuisance of himself by being generally loud and obnoxious. There was any number of these twats in every resort in Spain. There was something about being permanently on holiday that appealed to these lazy bastards and they paid for their scumbag lifestyle in any way they could. Running bets for local bar bookies, dealing in small quantities of recreational drugs for the local bigger dealer, and running up bar tabs with unsuspecting new bar owners (there was a never ending supply of these) and leaving them penniless whilst moving on to find another victim. Basically the lowest of the low, bottom feeding scum, worse than cockroaches, you get the idea.

Mostly Mack ignored Big Phil. He didn't deal in the bar and, by and large, Big Phil ignored him back. The thing is though, Big Phil didn't actually like being ignored. The cocaine and beer gave him an unnatural buzz that made him think he was king of the castle and centre of his own universe.

On this sunny afternoon Mack was sat at a table outside on the pavement with his new girlfriend Jill. They had just been to the local motorcycle shop to buy matching helmets for the scooter and were just enjoying a quiet moment in the afternoon heat. Big Phil came out of the bar and Mack briefly noticed him out of the corner of his eye. They rarely engaged each other with so much as a word but on this occasion Big Phil stopped by Mack's table.

"You've never liked me have you?" Big Phil's face was a mixture of anger and menace. "As it happens I haven't but I'm sure I'm not alone in that" Mack's manner was neutral but internally his finger was on the launch control button. Without further provocation Big Phil kicked Mack's table sending glasses, bottles and ice cubes flying. Jill was knocked over but luckily Mack was sat to one side and immediately jumped to his feet. "Oh, fancy your chances do you?" said the lanky fuck-wit. He held his arms out with the palms upwards in a 'come on then' manner. Mack never believed in pointless conversation with these wankers, he simply stepped in and punched Big Phil straight in the nose. Amazingly this had little effect.

It turned out that Big Phil's girlfriend had realized what a useless wanker he really was and walked out on him that morning. By way of solace Phil had embarked on a binge of drink and cocaine starting a 10AM and still apparently ongoing. By the time he engaged Mack he was high as a kite on sorrow, anger, bitterness, vodka and cocaine. He would be impervious to pain and full of endless energy. By all accounts he had already been in a couple of other bars having put a cigarette out in somebody's face and kicked a few more tables over.

To Mack's eternal amazement, what Phil did next would amuse him for years. Phil picked up one of the plastic terrace chairs (about 2Kg and flexible) and told Mack "I'm going to hit you with this." No accounting for drink and drugs when it comes to bad decision making. Phil swung the chair all the way to the side clearly intending to use it to hit Mack with. Well, to Mack this was almost slow-motion. Actually it was slow-motion. Both the chair and Phil's arms were swung round to the side as Mack moved forward stepping into a right hand hammer blow that started at his right heel, through his twisting hip, through his twisting shoulder and landed with devastating force right on the jaw bone of the chair wielding thug. Nothing; I mean NOTHING. Phil was staggered backwards but generally he should have been down, gone, out for the count, history. But no, as suspected this was going to take more, a lot more. As he staggered backwards Phil pickup a beer bottle from a table and flew at Mack. As easy as you like, Mack stepped to one side and Phil flew by. As Phil was off balance Mack kicked him behind the knee and he went down. Mack wasn't going to risk going to the ground with the wanker so he waited until he was getting to his feet. He then drew his knee virtually to his chin and delivered a driving kick to the side of Phil's knee. The knee collapsed at an unnatural angle and Phil fell to the ground screaming. Drugs or not, he wasn't getting up from that.

Mack walked over to his girlfriend to check on her and then they both got on his scooter and left. Phil was on crutches for three months. He saw Mack a few weeks later. "Listen man, I owe you an apology, I got what I deserved. When I am sorted I am going back to the UK and trying to straighten myself out. This place is bullshit". "Takes a man to apologise" said Mack, "no hard feelings". They shook hands and never spoke again.

This was also one of the reasons why Mack didn't spend so much time in ex-pat bars. They attracted

Brits of all persuasions, good and bad. If you were an average Joe, not bothering anybody, you would not really get involved with the seedier side of the clientele. However, if you were a tall, athletic, good looking bloke you could become something of a challenge, a magnet to the wankers. Mack wanted a quieter life, plus he enjoyed the more authentic atmosphere in Spanish bars further inland. He didn't understand the banter between the locals. The Spanish accent in Andalucía in general was like going to Glasgow to learn English; almost impossible to understand. But they were obviously just like blokes in bars in any part of the world. Clearly calling each other all the names under the sun, swearing and cursing and letting their hair down. Spanish culture was very macho. You did get women in bars but not many ladies.

Mack would take Jill for a quiet drink in a few local bars where the Spanish locals made them welcome with a *'hola'* and *'buenas tardes'.* Mack would reply likewise but that was about all he could manage at this stage. He was working on it though and, knowing Mack, he would get there sooner rather than later.

CHAPTER 12

By the front door

The weekly training sessions in the *dojang* gave Mack renewed enthusiasm and he decided he must put the Estepona problem to bed. Here's what he knew:

Handforth intended to import 5 kilos of uncut heroin from Morocco (Mack didn't understand about the difference in the weight between purchase and sale)). He wanted to sell it, suitably cut, to the Ukrainians in Estepona. Handforth wanted Mack to bridge the gap and any tensions between the two parties.

Why Mack? Well it's a strange thing. When you are capable of handling yourself and have been known to use extreme violence you are seen as 'hard'. People who are criminals cannot envisage anyone who is 'hard' not being a criminal themselves. When you are 'hard' it is better for certain criminals that you are associated with them and will pay handsomely for the association. So, Mack had been approached by Lee Handforth because Mack must have criminal intent. Logical, right?

So despite the fact that he had every intention of

destroying both operations, he was trusted by one half of the proposed arrangement and, by association, the other side would be prepared to talk to him.

Mack drove back down the A7 in his M5 pulling off at the Estepona Norte exit and passed the Carrefour supermarket. Driving down the *paseo* he parked in the underground carpark. He already knew that the centre of operations for the Ukranians was a bar call the Caribbean Mermaid a couple of street back from the *paseo*. He had already been and scoped the place out; he knew there was muscle inside the door

Mack walked straight in, there were no obvious customers in the bar only a couple of half shaven big lumps (they didn't seem to come in any other flavour these Ukrainians). Inside, the Caribbean Mermaid had clearly been neglected for some time. There were stains on the walls and the floor, the tiled bar had tiles missing and the stainless-steel counter had dents in it. The table had old dirty glasses on them and there were only a couple of bottles of vodka behind the bar.

Acting as if he had just wandered in off the street he strolled up to the bar and looked around for someone who was serving. Clearly, in this place bar staff was hard to come by, no-one appeared to be tending to the customers. "Hi guys, anyone serving in here" he asked casually. He never failed to wonder how the lowlife scum wanted to decide who could come and go or who could get a drink in a bar that they didn't own.

Sure enough, a grey skinned thug snuck up to him and getting way too close asked him "what you want?". Mack had no time for niceties or dickheads. "OK let's not mess about I want to speak with your boss, now fuck off and fetch him!" The ferocity of the reply and the direct eye contact took the thug aback. He was used to intimidating people not being threatened or stood up to. "Why you want to speak my boss?" he sneered. "Absolutely none of your fucking business now fuck off and tell him I want to see him". The arsewipe was basically used to taking orders so he went off to a room in the back looking back at Mack with a sneer.

After a minute a much larger version of the first tosser came out of the back and straight up to Mack. "Who the fuck are you?" The boss's English was heavily accented but grammatically better than normal. His attitude was one of superiority and suggested that Mack had better have a fucking good reason for disturbing him. To the boss's surprise Mack smiled and held out his hand. "Jack McClean, people call me Mack". The boss looked at Mack's outstretched hand and made an executive decision. Taking Mack's hand he said "Piotr, people call me Pete. Lots of people think I'm called Vlad but that's a local joke. Come; tell me how I can help you".

This was clearly a man of business, legal or otherwise, and someone Mack could deal with - before he destroyed his operation. Piotr was a big specimen easily as tall as Mack but a bit thicker set, no doubt he could dish it out if required. And in the thug's world, dishing it out was the measure of your worth; pretty much as it was in any criminal network throughout the world. It was all they understood, they were never going to win a debating contest.

"Thanks mate, I'm actually here on behalf of someone else, Lee Handforth, heard of him?" "Ah, the fat man in Puerto Banús no?" said Pete (or Piotr or Vlad or whatever his real name was) "The very one" said Mack. "He was wondering if you were interested in some product he was looking to distribute?"
"I suppose this product is something we need to talk about carefully no?" It didn't take much working out that they were singing off the same hymn sheet. "Correct" said Mack. "He is just waiting for a window to take the shipment and will be looking for a quick sale. He doesn't want direct contact for obvious reasons so has asked me to deal with you and set up the trade."

The Ukrainian regarded Mack carefully. This was an evil drug dealing thug and he wanted to remain an evil drug dealing thug for a lot longer. He certainly wasn't about to simply accept that Mack was who he said he was. Up to this moment neither party had mentioned anything illegal and had used their words guardedly. "How do I know you are who you say?" asked the boss. "Personally I don't give a fuck who you think I am" said Mack "I will tell you this though, I don't like walking in here and dancing around till you decide if I'm for real. You have a simple choice; I will call Handforth, you ask him what you want and then make a decision OK?"

Naturally it wasn't every day that a stranger simply walked in and offered illegal class A drugs for sale. So it wasn't surprising that they would want some sort of reassurance. Mack kicked himself, he should have been more prepared for this. Now he had no option but to call Handforth and he had a feeling how that was going to go down with the lovely friendly fat fucker. Mack dialled Handforth's number and waited for him to answer "Hi boss, I got a bit of a situation here and I need you to speak to our friend". Before Handforth could say anything he handed the phone to Piotr. The Ukrainian introduced himself and explained that he wasn't happy just taking Mack's word. How could he know this was on the level? Handforth equally was unhappy dealing directly with the Ukrainian. Mack was supposed to be the go-between and no direct contact, especially by phone was acceptable. "Let me speak to Mack" said Handforth. The boss man handed the mobile to Mack "What the fuck is this!" shouted Handforth down the phone so that everyone in the room had no doubt as to what was being said. "I don't deal directly with these cunts, that's your job! Now fucking sort it out!" "I don't think this is any different if it was the other way round" said Mack quite calmly, "how can I convince them that I am your official rep? I need something to give them". "OK tell him that I know that he is in business with someone whose initials are MS that's all he is going to get otherwise he can fuck off". One of the things with mobile phone is that you can't slam the handset down to end a call in anger however Mack could picture an expensive mobile phone being launched across Handforth's office.

The tension in the room had gone up several notches and Mack could see he had better sort this out now or he could be out of his depth. "Right, I don't know if this means anything but obviously we need to be careful with information given on the phone right? So, do the initial MS mean anything to you, Handforth says he is one of your business contacts and my guess is that this information is sensitive and known only to a few select people in the business correct?" The thug pondered a moment whilst Mack's internal mechanism engaged first gear with his hand firmly on the gearstick. "OK, more than a lucky guess I think; this is something that I understand. Please tell Mr Handforth that I apologise for the mistake and I will never contact him again". Mack relaxed if only a bit and tried to show outwardly that this was normal procedure for him.

"OK, no emails, texts or phone calls, we can't be too careful as you know. I will be back with more information nearer the time" Mack stood and went out of the bar and walked casually down the street although inside he was breathing a huge sigh of relief. He was dabbling in a world of extreme violence and suspicion; it didn't take much for things to go pear-shaped. And if it did go pear-shaped he wanted to be the one who started it. He knew from good experience that these idiots did not expect the violence to be started from a go-between, after all these were supposed to be the ones that kept everything running smoothly no? Well – usually.

CHAPTER 13

"How much? "

ow much was the quantity and how much was the price per Kg was what Mack needed to know. Not because he was going to sell or deliver any heroin but because he had to at least be seen to set the deal up. He was also interested in the machinery of the deal and the networks used by the filthy arsewipes who peddled misery for a living. Mack always wondered how you could be so far removed from reality or so cold hearted that it mattered not what the consequences of your actions were. All these motherfuckers knew was easy money and lots of it. Well there would be consequences; they just didn't know it yet.

The Ukraine produced some big specimens. God only knows what they fed them on but your typical Ukrainian thug was a big lump. The thing was, however, Mack had come across big lumps before. Most thugs were lazy bastards who didn't want to put the hard yards in when building muscle, so they took steroids - lots. Steroids grew muscle but it wasn't real hard strong muscle, it was just for show. Furthermore, it made them heavy without real strength to support their huge frames. So basically they looked the part to the general public they wanted to impress but to Mack they were nothing but immobile wankers who went down like sacks of potatoes when you smacked them.

It was the same with big fat fuckers. For some reason they used their size to appear strong and hard. They were usually strong; they had to be to carry that bulk around. If you kept out of harms reach (or arms reach) however, they had the stamina of a sloth and the speed of an earthworm. All show no go.

Mack turned up at the office of Lee Handforth. Well, not so much an office as a litter strewn dump above a bar in Puerto Banús,

Puerto José Banús, in the city of Marbella, was an enigma. The harbour was full of the most opulent yachts, many with permanent staff, some with helicopter pads, true high end luxury. In years gone by you would find the King of Saudi Arabia visiting. He owned two mansions on Marbella's 'Golden Mile' and had contributed heavily to the building of the main hospital on the Costa del Sol. Property prices in Puerto Banús were the most expensive on the coast along with the luxury apartments on the 'Golden Mile'.

Surrounding the leisure harbour were shops, bars and restaurants. Shops such as Dolce & Gabanna, Hermes, Chanel and the like. You could choose fine dining or more casual fare. You could not enter the harbour area in a car without a permit to get through the barrier and then you could park next to the bars and restaurants in your Porsche, Ferrari, McLaren or Bentley. An 'E' class Mercedes would be considered down market in this company. This was in-your -face luxury. Behind this facade however, was an underbelly rotten with corruption. It was not unusual for a two or three million euro cruiser to change hands for hard cash. The likes of Lee Handforth enjoyed the opulent surroundings and loved to be seen in Sinatra's Bar or The Red Tomato with some cheap hangers-on. Swilling Cristal champagne, which he didn't really like, and nodding to other low-life scum who wanted to be associated with the hoi poloi. Puerto Banús, didn't care whether you had old money, new money or dirty money; it was simply the money that counted.

Mack knocked lightly and let himself in. Handforth was on the phone with another arsehole, shouting into his mobile and very red in the face "I don't care what he says, I want that fucking money and I want it NOW! Smack him till he gives you summat. Next time he doesn't pay he is going to get wasted OK!" He clicked off the call and looked at Mack. "You just can't get the staff you know" he said in a false posh accent grinning and showing his tobacco stained teeth. "Good morning my friend, do we have good news?"

"Well it looks pretty straight forward" said Mack.

"They are happy to talk business and I am dealing directly with Vlad or Piotr of Pete or whatever he is called".

"Spot on, I've got the goods coming on Friday. I need to process it and package it so Sunday is a good day. I've got three kilos coming, that will be five kilos when I have finished with it. It's easy to work out the price. They sell it for a tenner a wrap which is a tenth of a gram so they want to be paying thirty euros a gram. Five kilos, I want hundred and fifty grand in Euros." That's a lot of hard moolah are you OK with that? "Don't you worry about a thing" said Mack. "How much are you paying then?" "None of you fucking business and don't ask again" sneered the fat cunt. Mack smiled "OK, OK just asking, I've got the message"

Mack now had his information to start planning to shut these two operations down. He was only going to get one chance at this and as skilled as he was he would be up against some seriously nasty arseholes. He headed back to Fuengirola to nurse bottle of *Mahou* and contemplate his fate.

CHAPTER 14

"Are you listening?"

The traditional martial arts were a mystery to the general public and, brought up on a diet of Kung-Fu movies, they believed if you practiced the martial arts you were capable of defending yourself and subduing any opponent. Nothing could be further from the truth.

Mack had never taken a backward step, especially with bullies and thugs. Since dealing with the boy in his first year at school he had dedicated himself to being the best he could be at Karate. However he soon found out it meant nothing out there in the real world.

In the dojo you practice moves, punches, strikes and kicks. You improve flexibility and fitness and you practice katas. You practice kumite by sparring with others of similar age and ability and you learn how to score points in competition. The problem with *kumite* in competition however is that, once a point is scored, the contest is stopped and you return to the middle of the mat, give a small bow and start again. All very organised and regulated. Absolutely no good whatsoever in the real world where thugs came in windmilling with bottles ,glasses or whatever was at hand. You had to learn to adapt the skills learned in the *dojo* into a real life situation.

At school however, people get to know you go to the local Karate club. To bullies this is a challenge that cannot be resisted. Especially when you are two or three years older that the potential victim. Next to Mack's school was a field where the kids used to go for a kick around at lunchtime. Mack was chatting with a couple of friends when a known big mouth from two years above him came towards him. "Oy, *Hong Kong Fuey*!" said the boy. "Show us some Kung Fu then" he said grinning. "I don't do Kung Fu" said Mack. "I don't give a fuck what you do, show me!" the boy was leaning in to Mack's face and doing his best 'hard man' look. "I'm not allowed to use it outside" said Mack, hoping the wanker would just go away. "Are you fucking listening?" said the boy, "show me some fucking whee ha or I'll knock you the fuck out!"
Now, we know Mack was stubborn; he was also full sure he would not be a puppet for this arse-hole or, for certain, this episode would have no end. "You'd better get on with it then" said Mack, preparing himself for the worst. What he didn't expect was the blow from behind from one of the hangers-on. This stunned him and he had little de-fence for the onslaught that followed. His mates

could do little to help him and he could only protect himself as best he could as the blows rained down. Luckily a sixth former saw the fracas and ran to break it up.

Mack was battered and bruised but he had received a life lesson that was to serve him well for the rest of his life. His martial arts had been of no use in that situation. You could be a one thousand Dan Super Kung Fu Grand Master with fists of fury but if someone put a bar stool round the back of your head you were toast. The boy didn't face him and bow. Rules didn't apply, there was no referee to stop the contest and their punches and kicks didn't count as points.

Mack's dad had also given him a great life lesson that would prove true in numerous situations. "When there are a group of bullies, there is always only one mouthpiece and the others are just hanging on. Drop the mouthpiece and the others will disappear, if you don't the others join in and make it worse". "Oh, and never, ever let them use their mouth as an advantage. Get in first and get in HARD". We now know that Mack had listened well.

Mack had been no sport for the bully and he generally left him alone apart from the odd *'Hong Kong Fuey'* jibe. In fact he didn't see him again once the boy had left school the following year.

Years later one Friday evening, Mack was having a quiet beer in town with a couple of friends, one of which had been there at the historic event. Mack and his friends would go on a pub crawl but Mack would be sensible with his alcohol, either taking a low alcohol beer or a fizzy water in between a bottle of premium lager. He had seen too many drunks and faced more than one of them not to know how alcohol affected your reactions and decision making. Mack could get merrily drunk in the right company but never around the town centre where idiots seemed to come out of the woodwork on a Friday and Saturday night.

Out of the corner of his eye Mack spotted the fuckwit from school. His hackles rose but he reigned in the red mist in favour of a quiet night out with his mates. In fact it was his mate who said to him "have you seen who's over there?" "yeah" said Mack, "he'd better behave himself". Unfortunately, bullies rarely change their spots. They love the dominance of insulting and intimidating people, especially to show off in company. Indeed the arsewipe spotted Mack across the room and his eyes lit up. "Oy, Hong Kong Fuey, how are yer!" he was grinning and mumbling to the group he was standing with; a couple of decent looking girls and another bloke.

He couldn't help himself, "show us some moves then!" he said laughing, clearly remembering his moment of glory and which he had clearly related to his assembled company. Mack chose to look away which the idiot took to be a sign of weakness and decided to pursue the matter. Walking over to

Mack he said "aren't you listening?" at least that is what he started to say. All he managed was "aren't y..." when Mack chopped him in his throat. The bar was quite crowded so roundhouse kicks were not an option. No matter, Mack proceeded to pummel his head and face. Such was the speed and ferocity of the assault nobody had any chance to react to prevent severe damage to the loudmouth. Leaving him unconcious Mack walked out of the bar into the cool fresh air with a big weight off his shoulders. His mate said " I never liked that bar, it's a bit rough". Mack laughed and put his arm round his mate's shoulder, "come on pal, let's go down the Golden Lion"

Indeed, what Mack had learned in the intervening years was that street fighting had nothing in common with the *dojo*. What the martial arts did give you however was speed, accuracy and power. The ability to get in first, get in hard and not to stop until the job was done. And the job was to ensure they did not get up and they did not come back for more, now or in the future.

CHAPTER 15

"Think you're hard do you?"

Home life for Mack was ideal. He lived in the Idle area of Bradford which was a decidedly middle class area. A mixture of traditional stone terraces and newer brick built semi-detached houses. A couple of decent pubs with Sky Sports and Pub Grub were within walking distance and his dad made use of both of them. He lived with his mum and dad and his older sister Carol. Carol was a few years older than Mack and in typical fashion she thought he was a being from another planet. She wasn't the sporty type and was preparing for her A levels and starting to look at her University options. Before too long she would be off to Uni and Mack could occupy her larger bedroom although the 'Barbie' wallpaper may have to go. So rather than cherishing his older sister, he couldn't wait for her to bugger off – charming no?

Mack dad Joe worked as a builder, he had been a professional rugby league player in his younger days having played as a centre for Bradford Bulls and Dewsbury. When Mack's dad played for the Bulls they were known as Bradford Northern, a reference to the original name for the game, The Northern Rugby Football Union. After 1996 the game had become known as 'Superleague' and most of the clubs had adopted NFL style names such as Wolves, Tigers and Warriors; not to everyone's taste but times change.

He had been quite a name around town and often featured in the sports pages of the Bradford 'Telegraph and Argus' newspaper. But rugby league professional weren't like soccer players; they were celebrities of sorts but by and large they were still part of their local communities. It wasn't unusual for Mack's dad to be in his local pub after a game with the locals ribbing him about dropping a pass or praising him for scoring a great try.

What the game of rugby league had given Mack's dad however was the attitude to never take a backward step or to walk away from confrontation. He had the focussed mind of a professional sportsman and this clearly rubbed off on the young Mack as well as giving him the genetic make-up to go with it.

Mack played soccer at school. His dad would have liked Mack to join a rugby league club but he was clearly dedicated to his martial arts and as long as he was physically active his dad left him to it. He knew that; if you pushed someone in a particular direction they would usually push back. Plus, he was clearly very good at Karate and, on the occasions he met his *sensei* he received glowing reports about his son. Mack would make his dad proud in his martial arts achievements.

Mack's mum Janet was a hairdresser and owned her own salon by the traffic light in Greengates, just around the corner from the family home. Mack would call in on his way home from school for a coffee. The old dears having their perms would fuss over the handsome young boy which made Mack blush but he liked it as well. He also received free haircuts and his mum could practice her modern styles on Mack so he always looked well groomed. Even today Mack kept up with his appearance and his hair was always well trimmed.

One Saturday morning Mack had been out with his dad who was pricing a job for a client. The weather was typical Bradford drizzle although, having never known any different it was just normality for Mack. Weather was weather and you couldn't do anything about it. As they say; there is no such thing as bad weather, only bad clothing.

As they came back to the car Mack heard a voice shout out "Oy McClean you wanker have you given up dropping passes now?" The gobshite was addressing his dad and was clearly drunk even at this time of day. Mack wasn't sure what to make of this but his dad simply smiled at the man and pressed the remote to unlock the car. "I never rated you, you cunt, thought you were shit at the Bulls" The man was grinning and did a quick double step to maintain his balance. Mack's dad looked down at his son and saw the slightly shocked look on his face. His dad had taken his share of banter over the years but most of it was good natured from genuine fans of the game. This however was a step too far. Mack's dad skirted around the back of the car and walked up to the man. The man was about to say something like "you think you are still hard do you?" but all he managed was "you think….." as Mack's dad planted a beauty right on his chin. The man was out like a light. Laid in a puddle, wet through with onlookers all thinking he just got what he deserved. Nobody rang for the police or ambulance.

Mack's dad simply walked back to the car packed the groceries and drove off. Turning to Mack he said "sorry about that son. Sometimes you just can't let it go. And remember; never let them use their mouth. Get in first and get in hard."

Mack was proud as punch of his dad. That's the way to deal with wankers.

CHAPTER 16

Swish, Bang

Handforth was coy about the delivery; this was a key part of his operation. He had other activities which involved distributing cannabis and cocaine as well as a nightclub in Fuengirola and a sex shop on 'Sin Alley', an area of Fuengirola where you could satisfy your most base desires.

It was through the nightclub that Handforth had come to know Mack. Mack worked occasionally as a doorman to earn a few euros plus, the half-dressed girls that came through the door were a great source of comfort from time to time. The head of security had mentioned Mack to Handforth as being particularly handy when needed.

Mostly Mack had to watch out for predatory young Spaniards and Moroccans bothering the young British and Scandinavian girls. The girls had a habit of 'pre-loading', chugging a couple of bottles of 'Prosecco' down before leaving the hotel. This meant they didn't need to spend too much on drinks in the club and they would encourage the boys to buy them cocktails. The cocktails were much stronger than they could often handle and the next thing was you had a twenty year old puking and falling over, all bra and knickers (if they were even wearing a bra). Mack would encourage her to get in a taxi with her friends, ensuring that they set off before going back inside to deal with the next minor incident. There were rarely any fights inside the club and all the boys were patted down on entry to check for weapons. It was a thing with the modern generation, if they weren't carrying a blade they did not feel so 'hard' and were not fond of old fashioned fist fights. If a couple of boys were getting a bit lairy Mack only had to intervene with a gentle word. At work he wore a skin tight black 'Lycra' t-shirt and it showed he was definitely not one to be messed with. It also attracted admirers among the young ladies.

If there were any more shenanigans from the lads Mack would simply escort them to the door. He didn't care what they did to each other outside.

One night in summer when the nightclub area of Fuengirola was really busy with kids on holiday, partying until dawn, Mack noticed a couple of Moroccans mixing with the kids outside the nightclub clearly selling illegal 'highs'. Mack knew full well this went on and obviously nobody could dance all night without pharmaceutical assistance. The trouble was; he hated Moroccans. To Mack they were worse than Bradford Asians. At least in Bradford, the Asians had a historic right to be there. Their parents and grandparents had been actively encouraged to come and do the jobs that white people no longer wanted to do.

These Moroccans however were opportunist predators selling anything of any quality to kids who had no idea what they were taking from cunts who couldn't care less what the drugs did to their minds and bodies.

On this occasion Mack wandered casually over to The Moroccans who were pretending to the new best friend of a group of scarcely dressed teenage girls. "Listen mate, just fuck off OK. If you want to sell your shit do it somewhere else". The Moroccan, who looked like an unwashed streak of shit said" " I don't fuck off, you fuck off or I make a phone call fucking bastard" Always cocky and sure of their status as untouchable these cocksucking fuckers managed to take Mack from calm to murderous in zero seconds flat.

The main entrance to the 'Heaven's Door' nightclub was actually simply that, a doorway rising out of the plaza allowing entrance to the underground club. Behind it was an empty area with just a few smokers hanging around. Mack grabbed the stick insect by the neck and dragged him round the back of the doorway. The security manager saw this and headed round to make sure Mack was OK. By the time he got there the Moroccan was unconscious with his nose plastered over his face.

"Everything OK Mack?" "yeah, just a misunder-standing" said Mack. At this moment a second Moroccan came running round the corner and, seeing his partner, pulled a knife saying "I kill you!" - big mistake.

The security manager said to Mack "leave it, we'll sort him out another time". Mack took no no-tice. The Moroccan strode towards Mack with the knife held in front of him. These idiots didn't ac-tually train to fight with knives, they usually just showed them and people backed off so the useless waster did exactly the wrong thing, he swung the knife in an arc looking to slash anything in the way. The problem with that is; once you missed (which he did) the knife was now on the outside of the arc and pointing at nothing. Lots of people see the movies and believe you can catch the knife arm and disable the attacker; very dangerous. The Moroccan was pretty quick. He intended to swing the knife twice, inside to out and outside to in, 'swish swish' but all he managed was 'swish'. With incredible timing and accuracy Mack smashed the cockroach between the eyes. So now he was stunned and also couldn't see, better than trying to catch his arm no?

What happened next was not for the faint hearted because, now he did catch the knife arm, twisting viciously and putting the arsewipe on his knees. He wasn't looking to disarm the cunt he simply kept twisting until snapping sounds and screams were heard. He then took the limp knife hand with the knife in if and pushed the knife into the free hand of the helpless shithead and then Mack got close to the ear of the blubbering Moroccan, "listen cunt, I'll kill you and anyone else that thinks they can deal on my manor, GOT IT!" then he sparked him with a vicious blow to the side of the temple. Even the security manager had to look away at this point. Mack walked away, his heart rate already approaching normal.

So, this is how Mack came to the attention of Lee Handforth. The security manager was handy in his own right but he had seen that Mack was a different animal. And as we have noted before, if you are seen to be 'hard' you must be a criminal right?

So Mack had worked his way into Handforth's inner circle. Handforth told him "I'm sending the gear down on Friday. Be here at 10 o'clock and see it gets to where it needs to and then you collect the cash and get back here OK?" "Sorted" said Mack, everything was falling into place.

CHAPTER 17

"It had better be good"

Mack now knew the amount of heroin and the price. He needed to make contact with the Ukrainians again and couldn't risk a phone call. So, once again he made his way down the A7 listening to his favourite compilation of mixed soul and Northern Soul. 'Time Will Pass You By' by Toby Legend had just finished. One of the three final tracks played at the legendary Casino Club in Wigan, Lancs before it burned to the ground in 1981.

Mack wasn't old enough to have attended personally but his Dad and his friends had spent many a night dancing to the frantic rhythm of rare American soul records. Through his dad's record collection he had grown up with a great advantage and had come to appreciate the quality and rarity of some fantastic tunes that had never had commercial success. Not in the UK anyway. The scene continued to thrive in its own small way and Mack was on the lookout for other aficionados on the coast.

Next on the sound system was 'Do I Love You' by

Frank Wilson, one of the rarest 45 rpm singles on the planet. Brilliant driving beat and fantastic Motown backing. As the track was playing the music was interrupted by the on board Bluetooth phone system. He looked at the display to see it was his girlfriend Jill calling. He pressed the green phone button on the steering wheel and said "hello love". Jill was the lady who had witnessed Big Phil being disabled and Mack was grateful he had not needed to be too violent in dealing with him (apart for putting him on crutches for three months). He never wanted people he cared about seeing him at his worst. Jill had filled a hole in his life that, truth be known, nothing could really fulfil. She was making a good attempt though. Beautiful and funny, she was an Essex girl with blond hair, blue eyes and a need to party.

"Hiya babes", she had that unmistakeable Eastend accent. "What you up to?". "Not much love, just driving down the coast to see an old mate in Casares" "Where's that then?" She had that wonderful quality of being blissfully unaware of the geography of the coast or, in fact, where anywhere was. She thought Scottish people were simply from the north of England, a fact that annoyed the living daylights out of any Scottish people she came across. She wound the Scottish up even further when she said "well, we are all just one country aren't we?" You couldn't be mad at her for long though when she lit up the room with her stunning smile. "It's a little white village up in the hills above Estepona" said Mack, knowing that meant nothing to his beautiful airhead. "Oh, I'd love to see it. Do they have sangria there?" "Yes dear, believe it or not you can get sangria all over Spain" Mack smiled at her naivety.

"Are we going out for a Chinese later?" she asked. "Yeah, can do. I might need a beer or two as it happens. I'll give you a bell later on". "Oh, alright darling, see you later, love you" "You too" said Mack. Jill said "love you" all the time. He wasn't sure if it meant anything in the deeper sense but he did care for her a lot. Time would tell, he was in no rush.

He pulled into Estepona, parked up and found himself walking into the Caribbean Mermaid without breaking stride. "Is he in" asked Mack to the nearest grey skinned thug. "In back" said the surly wanker. Mack walked through to find Piotr/Pete/Vlad nursing a bottle of vodka with a label he had never seen before. "Mack" said the boss man. "Tell me, what's the score? You want vodka?" "Not at this hour of the day thanks" said Mack. "I'll keep this short then I'll fuck off if you don't mind? I'll be down on Friday with 5 kilos of gear. My man will come in with the gear, leave it and walk straight out. When I see everything is clear I will come and collect the cash. Hundred and fifty grand grand in used notes OK?" Pete looked at Mack with an intense stare. "I will need to test it before I give you money but won't take long. If everything OK I will pay you everything. If this is good stuff, and it had better be good, we can deal again when you had stuff no?" "Yeah why not?" said Mack. It was slightly amusing that the filthy cunt thought there might be a next time.

Mack left and set off for Fuengirola. This time he took the AP7 toll road that had been built in the 'noughties' when Spain was building a road and rail infrastructure that was unprecedented. The fact was that Spain was so far behind the rest of Europe following Franco's death that they needed to upgrade the road and rail network to 21st century standards. Countries like the UK could only look on in envy as Spain constructed thousands of miles of motorways, toll roads and high speed AVE rail links without contributing one 'centimo'.

Before the upgrade to the coast road and the subsequent toll road it had been a nightmare for tourist and residents to access Gibraltar and the large port of Algeciras. Actually it was only by coincidence that Gibraltar became more accessible. If the Spanish could have avoided it they would. There was no love lost between the British and Spain over the thorny subject of 'The Rock'. Many Brits who don't speak Spanish will not notice the wall surrounding the town of San Roque, (which you pass some 10 Km before arriving at the Rock) with the message emblazoned *Dónde vive los de Gibraltar'* - where the people of Gibraltar live. Not the people who live in Gibraltar now, no; where the people who were chucked out by the Brits three hundred years ago live. No bitterness there then!

As usual the AP7 was virtually deserted, nobody liked paying the tolls but it provided a fast link up and down the Costa del Sol, there weren't any speed cameras either so Mack floored the Beemer up to 150 KPH. He pulled off at the Mijas/Fuengirola exit and paid the toll at the barrier - over five euros. Expensive if you used it a lot but word was the government were going to abolish the tolls, probably to ease pressure on the toll free motorways.

Driving down the Mijas road towards Fuengirola he could see the Med shimmering in the distance. Behind him was the white village of Mijas overlooked by the Sierra de Mijas mountain range. This really was a beautiful place to live thought Mack, or it would be if there wasn't such a toxic underbelly. Work to be done, he thought, let the clean-up begin.

As he drove down into Fuengirola he called Jill on the hands free car phone. "Hi love, what time are we going out?" "I'll see you in the Majesty about seven OK?" Jill lived in a one bedroom apartment just off Church Square which was the British description of the *Plaza de la Constitution* the central part of downtown Fuengirola. The square was dominated by a traditional white church (obviously) with a bell tower.

Mack walked in to the Majesty about five to seven and ordered a bottle of *Mahou* from Danny the barman/owner. Jill waltzed in about ten past all smiles and jolliness. She was wearing the highest heels imaginable with a dress that just came below her waist. Her handbag was finished in silver glitter and she looked generally as if she was going to a party, which was how Jill looked every time she went out. "Hiya babes, you alright?" "All the better for seeing you" Mack replied giving her a peck on the cheek. He would have given her a kiss on the lips but the deep red lipstick wouldn't have gone with his outfit. "Grape juice?" he asked, which was Jill's description of white wine. "Oh go on then" she smiled. Everyone loved Jill, she lit up any room when she walked in and couldn't offend anyone if she tried, apart from Scottish people, of course, although that was simply inadvertent.

They had a couple of drinks and headed onto their favourite Chinese restaurant the 'New Dynasty'. The local Brits amusingly referred to the restaurant as the 'New Dysentery' although the food was actually very good, very cheap and no-one ever got ill from eating there. All Chinese restaurants in Fuengirola were similar in that they offered a set three course menu for under six euros which was incredible value for money.

They ordered a bottle of 'Tsingtao' Chinese beer for Mack and a glass of white wine for Jill. They ordered coffees to finish and the whole lot was under twenty euros – happy days.

Afterwards they wandered around a couple of tourist bars. Jill always attracted admiring glances and tonight was no different.

As they were sat outside the 'Dolphin' on Fish Alley, an area of Fuengirola which was wall to wall restaurants Mack got up to visit the gents. On his way back he saw a man at the bar that he knew and he stopped for a quick chat. Out of the corner of his eye he spotted that there was a bloke stood at his table talking to Jill. "Speak to you again" he said to the man at the bar and strolled outside. Just as he approached the table he heard the man, who was clearly drunk, saying "I think you're fucking gorgeous, I bet you're a great shag". Jill was trying not to make eye contact and was clearly uncomfortable. Across the road from the bar was a small alley with bins for the restaurants to use. Mack didn't break stride, he got hold of the idiot by the collar and dragged him across to the small alleyway. As he got hold of the drunk the man lost his footing but Mack simply physically dragged him the rest of the way. Out of sight of the bar and Jill Mack laid into the man and left him in a bloody heap. If you can't hold your beer don't drink it thought Mack.

He returned to Jill and gave her a big hug. "Sorry about that love, he won't bother you again" Jill was clearly shaken "where has he gone now?" She asked. "Oh, don't worry about him any more" said Mack "come on let's go round to the 'Tu Casa' which was another of their favourite bars. Jill soon came round to be her bubbly self and they finished the night off with a couple of *pacherans* a traditional aperitif from the north of Spain. Well, the *pacheran* wasn't quite the end of the night. They got a taxi back to Mack's place and finished the night off in style.

CHAPTER 18

"This is shit"

Mack had a couple of days to form a plan of attack (and attack it would be). He was forming a fire in his belly that would be unleashed in unprecedented fury at these scum-sucking shitbags. He knew that these fuckers were accustomed to violence but usually when dishing it out. Both parties thought he was a likeminded criminal who was simply facilitating a routine illegal trade. Both outfits would be super wary and Mack's attitude would need to be spot on. Truth be known, he had never done anything remotely like this before and he would need to act as if it was like water off a duck's back to him.

Mack knew there would be at least 5 Ukrainian thugs of varying sizes and experience in the Estepona bar. Forewarned and forearmed was the key. They just thought he was there as the money man, which he was. It's just that the money wasn't going to Handforth and the drugs weren't going out on the street.

On the Friday Mack turned up at ten to ten and grabbed a coffee. Handforth nodded at him and said "Jimmy is setting off in a minute, follow him to the drop and pick the dosh up will you?" "Yeah, no problem. I'll be straight back here after. Should be about an hour or so". Handforth appreciated the professional approach Mack gave to the job. He wasn't used to not having to spell out every step of the operation to numpties. "There's a nice little bonus for you when you get back". That could mean anything but it made no difference. Mack's bonus was going to be something the fat cunt was not anticipating.

Mack went out and got in his car and followed the lackey to Estepona down the A7 and to the Ukrainian's bar. 'Stick by me Baby' by The Salvadors was playing on the eight speaker Blaupunkt stereo. An absolute Northern Soul classic and Mack was tapping his fingers on the steering wheel contemplating his immediate future.

The A7 was a historic road formerly the N340 and still designated such in places. Parts of the road dated from Roman times and it allegedly had run From Cádiz to Rome. For most of its length it hugged the coast and provided beautiful views of the Mediterranean Sea. On a clear day you could see the rock of Gibraltar and on a really clear day you could see across to the coast of north Africa and the twin peaks of Ceuta, a Spanish enclave in north Morocco. Today it seemed incongruous with Mack's intentions; true beauty to shadow Mack's inner beast.

Mack realized by now that the Ukrainians must actually own the Caribbean Mermaid bar as no-one would tolerate this level of illegal activity without shitting their pants and blabbing to the police. Mack parked across the road and watched as Jimmy went in the bar and came out two minutes later. He looked up and down the street and checked for open windows and then got out and walked in the bar.

This was a typically tired traditional Spanish bar. there was a small terrace with plastic chairs emblazoned with the 'Estrella' logo, a brand of beer. The tables were tubular steel legs topped with Formica with similar branding. Inside there was a brick built bar faced with traditional Spanish tiles with patterns that resembled Christmas trees. Wooden chairs with spindle backs surrounded pine tables and there were crates both empty and full for various beverages, soft drinks and bottled beers. There was a single beer pump on the bar with the logo for 'Alhambra' beer; unsurprisingly a Granada brewery.

Mack was only wearing a Ralph Lauren copy polo shirt bought at the local market for ten euros. A couple of the thugs were wearing waistcoats and clearly packing something. Mack was aware there could be guns involved; but guns were only involved when things went pear-shaped and the gun carrier had time to do something about it.

Mack wandered into the back room without invitation. Pete the thug was opening up the package with a very sharp looking knife. Out of a drawer he took out a box that looked like prescription medication. Nowadays, of course, heroin could be checked for purity with official test kits. Authorities were more concerned with the quality of drug taken by addicts rather than the fact that addicts were taking the drug. At least this could prevent needless deaths.

Pete the thug dropped a couple of drops of the solution onto a small sample of the heroin. It turned a shade of brown and he compared this to a graded colour chart, this gave him the percentage of purity; in this case 40% pure. "This is shit" said the thug "but at least it is good shit" he smiled. Mack's heart skipped a beat, he had thought things were going to get messy before he was wanting it to.

Pete the thug nodded to an accomplice who opened a safe in the corner and took out a holdall. Handing it to Mack he said "count this". Mack looked in the bag which was packed with bundles of 50 euro notes. He now realized he should have a bank note counter. A proper outfit would have one and now he looked like an amateur. He had no way of telling if this was real of fake money. What the hell, he thought let's just get on with it.

He took the money out of the bag and counted it in thousand euro piles. Satisfied after about twenty minutes he put it back in the bag. "You can have the bag for free" said Pete the thug. Mack also realized he should have his own bag, his own money counter, rubber bands, the lot. He looked a twat in front of these seasoned gangsters. Nothing to be done, he stood up and left without saying a word. He went to his car and got in and drove it two streets round the corner.

He parked up and put a light jacket on, slipping his favourite wooden accessory up the sleeve. He had a plan of action as long as the thugs were still more or less where they were. Marching purposefully round to the bar Mack walked straight in. The first one with a waistcoat on was sat at the bar. Mack walked up to him slipping the pool cue out and pushing the screw end into his eye socket. As quick as anything he flipped it the other way and slammed it into the wanker's skull.

Now, you could train all you liked, you could have a twenty six inch neck, you could have a jaw of iron but you couldn't build bone on top of your head. No-one could resist the force that Mack used, the arsehole's skull caved in, end of story. Now speed was critical. Obviously the gang were aware that the game was afoot. There was one other thug in the bar area. He was just reaching into his pocket when Mack went to work. Throat, temple and back of the skull, out of the picture. Mack was now running into the back room. Only about five seconds had passed. No time to assess and react to the situation. The other waistcoat wearer was reaching into his vest. This put both arms out of commission, one holding the vest open the other reaching for the weapon. Mack drew the club over his head and brought it down with a devastating blow that ended the thug's sorry existence quicker than the poor victims of his evil trade. Two to go including Pete/Vlad/Piotr. Mack drove a side kick into the desk scattering papers and drugs, coffee, mobile phones anything else on the desk up in the air and knocking Pete backwards and out of reach of the desk drawer. Without breaking stride he hurled himself at the fourth henchman who by now had pulled a knife. Mack virtually ignored it, he smashed the cue onto his wrist instantly breaking it.

I don't care who you are, it is all but impossible to react with sufficient speed and authority to prevent an onslaught such as Mack was delivering. The thug screamed and dropped the weapon just as Mack smashed the cue into the side of his head and then broke his neck with a brutal downward blow of the cue. One left, Pete was only just gaining his feet when Mack drove the cue straight into his face. Many experienced fighters can parry kicks and punches but there is no defence for a direct strike through your guard, even if you have one. Pete was stunned and trying to windmill his arms. I don't care who you are, it is all but impossible to react with sufficient speed and authority to prevent an onslaught such as Mack was delivering. The thug screamed and dropped the weapon just as Mack smashed the cue into the side of his head and then broke his neck with a brutal downward blow of the cue. You would have had to have been there to witness the speed and ferocity that Mack was working with. The Ukrainians were hard bastards but they had never faced anything like this.

One left, Pete was only just gaining his feet when Mack drove the cue straight into his face. Many experienced fighters can parry kicks and punches but there is no defence for a direct strike through your guard, even if you have one. Pete was stunned and trying to windmill his arms to prevent more blows. Mack simply watched and with perfect timing whacked him round the ear. He then proceeded to smash his head to a bloody pulp. You would not recognize him by his passport photo now. DNA would be required to identify his body. Mack turned and noticed the safe was still open. Happy days. He found thousands of euros bagged up. The proceeds of misery. All Mack could do now was spend it happily.

He bagged up the money and the gear and left. As he walked round to his car a couple of tourist were walking past the bar. "Fancy a quick one before lunch dear?" said the plump man to his fat wife. This would be one to tell the kids about - when they had finished throwing up.

CHAPTER 19

Jessie Burgess

Steve Burgess was a bully. He had always been a bully. From an early age he had enjoyed intimidating people, insulting them for fun and beating them for no other reason than they stood out from the crowd. They could be a bit overweight, ginger, Asian or black, a bit spotty or absolutely any other tiny discrepancy from the norm. Known as Jessie for as long as he could remember nobody called him Steven or Steve. In fact people would say "do you know Jessie Burgess, he's fucking mental he is".

It wasn't a result of his upbringing or because he came from a broken family that he was a bully; you couldn't pin that social deprivation shit on Jessie. He had been brought up in a middle class family with both parents working in the hilltop village of Queensbury between Bradford and Halifax. No, Jessie was a bully because he enjoyed being a bully. Basically he was just a vicious arsehole.

Queensbury is one of the highest villages in England if not the highest. It was famous mainly for the Black Dyke Mills brass band which was a world class, award winning brass band originally associated with the Black Dyke mills, a worsted spinning mill owned by John Foster and Sons Ltd. People from Queensbury are a hardy bunch, the wind blows cold and the winters are harsh and Jessie didn't need to look far for a fight on a Saturday night.

Growing up Jessie lived in a semi-detached house on Roper Lane with views to die for looking across Halifax towards Elland and the Ainley Top motorway junction with the M62. To the right you looked towards the Pennines 15-20 miles in the distance. You were on the edge of the Yorkshire countryside and many walkers passed Jessie's house.

Jessie's parents were often at their wits end trying to understand their son. God only knows, they had tried. From an early age he had been wayward; his teachers often had to have words with his long suffering parents and pointing out his latest misdemeanour. He was forever being hauled in front of the head teacher where he simply stared at the floor whilst mumbling whatever it was they wanted to hear. He hated having to say he was sorry, because he wasn't, but sometimes they just went on and on and it was easier to say sorry than have them carrying on so. To Jessie it was slightly amusing really. Corporal punishment had long ago ceased to be an option for correctional purposes and Jessie had worked out that he could literally get away with murder (not actually, not just yet) and they could do fuck all about it. The most frustrating thing was that Jessie was quite bright. His junior school teachers breathed a collective sigh of relief when he passed the entrance exam to attend a particularly good school in Bradford and finally be rid of him. More than one of the male teachers, and probably the odd female one, would have love to leather young Jessie to teach him a lesson; but their hands were tied. They would lose their careers. Anyway he was gone now and good luck to his future mentors.

The Saturday night pub crawl around Queensbury was a tradition long established among the locals. You could start at either end; Queensbury stood on the old turnpike road between Halifax and Bradford and had a regular sprinkling of hostelries along the route. From Jessie's end on the Halifax side he would start in the Royal Oak before wending his merry way to the Omnibus, the New Dolphin and usually ending up in the Ring O' Bells. He had been barred several times from the Ring O' Bells but it was a rough pub anyway and he usually found his way back in by saying he was sorry; which, of course, he wasn't.

At school he was a particular nuisance as he continued to bully, insult and generally annoy the other pupils. He recalled one day he had spotted a second year pupil who, he had been told, fancied himself as a proverbial Bruce Lee and had started practicing karate. He thought it would be good sport to make him his puppet and make him show him some moves. He had had a laugh with the boy calling him *Hong Kong Fuey* which Jessie thought was funny. It turned out that the boy was not one to play his game and he had just ended up giving him a beating. The boy no longer interested Jessie.

The teachers were at their wits end and he had been referred to a social worker who specialized in behavioural problems. The problem with Jessie was that there were no psychological triggers for his behaviour, no nature/nurture debate plus he was particularly adept at appearing contrite and cooperative in his sessions. At heart he was a manipulative sociopath; he had no regard for the feelings of others and simply took great pleasure in hurting people.

Other pupils avoided him like the plague apart from a couple of other arseholes who thought it cool to be part of his entourage and the protection from retribution that it brought.

As he grew older he became more violent as well as finding that he could earn good pocket money by selling illegal highs such as E's and Ketamine. So it came to pass in his later teens that he was a drug dealing violent thug already forming the connections that would lead to bigger crimes and harder drugs.

He couldn't help himself when it came to bullying and intimidating people. One night, whilst out on the town in Bradford, he had spotted the little wanker from school who he had called *Hong Kong Fuey* although he hadn't been too much fun in the end. He was a bit bigger now but that didn't bother Jessie. He thought he would have some more fun with him now. He said to the small group he was with "watch this; I'm going to have a laugh with that tosser over there. He used to do Karate and he thinks he is something special" He thought the bloke had spotted him as he seemed to think he had just turned his head away. "Oy! *Hong Kong Fuey!* Show us some moves then!" He was laughing but the bloke didn't seem to be taking the bait. Jessie didn't like being ignored; no bully did. Fucking wanker, he thought, I'll show him and Jessie set off across the pub to have some fun.

He came round a few minutes later and found himself on the floor of the pub. He was pretty sure his jaw was broken. Jessie couldn't believe it; no-one did this to him. The only problem was, he didn't know where the bastard lived and didn't know how to get to him. One day, he thought, one day…

Jessie had been convicted a couple of times for small time dealing and on the second occasion he had been sentenced to four years in prison. He spent the time in HMP Armley in Leeds, a Victorian dump that had a reputation as a tough place to serve your time. For Jessie it was like going to college to study how to be a proper criminal. He had battled and fought and bitten and gouged his way to his two year early release. He didn't get released early for good behaviour; that was no longer the case in sentencing. Nowadays they just threw you out anyway and in Jessie's case, as was usual with him, they were over the fucking moon to see the back of him.

There was always the debate as to whether prison sentencing was meant to punish or rehabilitate. In Armley (in fact, in most incarceration facilities in the UK) it had long since ceased to be a punishment. Stupid left wing soft-in-the-head do-gooders had ensured that the inmates had all the facilities to make their stay as comfortable as possible. Also, sentencing nowadays was way too short to provide any sort of rehabilitation; even if there were the facilities. They had too few social workers with the necessary experience to deal with committed criminals. So Jessie had received not one second of assessment or therapy. The only thing Armley had done for him was to form alliances with proper high-end evil doers and, on release, he was straight away in contact with heroin dealers, pimps and enforcers from the seedier side of Leeds. In this environment he thrived. He wasn't the full-on super crook that would run such an operation but he was an extremely handy henchman who would have no issue going where directed to dish out drugs, punishment or whatever was asked of him. Such was his tendency to be a deliverer of mindless violent assault that his bosses provided him with an illegal pistol which he carried with him with personal pride. He could be relied upon to use whatever methods necessary to get the job done. A bullet in the knee or brain, it didn't make any difference to Jessie. He was so attached to his weapon that he risked carrying it with him at all times.

CHAPTER 20

"Oy, Hong Kong Fuey!"

So, how had Mack ended up on the Costa del Sol and what drove him to deal with these thugs in such a brutal way?

Well, that's two questions. Firstly, Mack came to the Costa del Sol three years ago. He had had a long term relationship in the UK with a stunning looking partner. She was all he had ever wanted and he had every intention of marrying her when the time was right, which would be soon.

He had come to be the Sales Director of a major franchised motor dealer selling Mercedes Benz vehicles. He had a high end Mercedes company car and other benefits commensurate with an important position such as he held.

He was young to hold such a position but actually he had been head-hunted for the position through his reputation in the trade. Through endless networking he had developed contacts both in and out of the trade. He had contract-hire clients taking hundreds of vehicles each year and repeat private clients by the dozen.

In his new position he could develop these contacts whilst building new business contacts for his team to deal with. As director he was responsible for Key Performance Indicators in terms of profit, finance targets, accessory sales targets among others. This was new to Mack but, as expected, he took everything in his stride.

Mack still attended the gym regularly and kept himself in peak physical condition. In the gym he concentrated on 'spinning', bag work and lots of reps with light weights. If you wanted to build muscle you needed to lift weights beyond your natural ability and effectively 'rip' muscle which would then repair and gradually build upon itself. For strength lots of reps built muscle fibre within existing muscle. This gave surprising strength in a smaller frame. This was how a lightweight boxer would train and how a female athlete could show amazing power. Mack wasn't lightweight but he wasn't a huge lump either. Seventeen and a half stone (245lb) but with enormous muscle density, Mack could deliver a straight punch or a kick with devastating effect. Along with the speed, focus and accuracy he possessed he rarely needed more than two blows to sort most opponents out. If he needed more than two blows it was because his opponent (or victim) had really pissed him off. Any more than two blows was basically punishment.

He ate in good restaurants when he dined out, which was not often and he had a local pub he used although occasionally he would still venture into town on a Saturday night.

One Saturday he had taken his partner Donna into town with a couple of friends and they were stood in a bar quietly chatting away. His mate said to him "hey Mack, what did they call the first Paki off the boat?" "Fuck me that's an old one" said Mack. "Amir!" As old as it was they still laughed. Out of the corner of his eye he spotted a movement and turning he saw a gun pointed at him. Holding the gun was the bully from school who Mack had humiliated some years ago and who had subsequently descended into scumland becoming a local drug dealer and enforcer. "Oy, *Hong Kong Fuey*! Who's the hard man now eh?" Mack saw the trigger being pulled and immediately ducked whilst moving towards the cunt. The low-life squeezed off a couple of shots in Mack's general direction creating panic in the pub as everyone jostled to get out of the way. This knocked the thug off-balance and Mack saw his chance. Leaping at the wanker Mack buried his fist into the thug's temple stunning him. He grabbed the gun arm and twisted viciously snapping tendons and releasing the weapon. Mack then grabbed the fucker around the neck and took him to the ground. Using a killer hold and using one arm as a lever he tightened his grip until the would-be murderer's neck snapped. Mack was already strong but in this instance the adrenaline rushing through his veins gave him superhuman strength.

At the same time two local bobbies entered the bar as Mack got to his feet. His first thought was as to the safety of his friends and Donna. Looking across he saw his friends crouched over a figure on the floor. Running across he saw Donna laid out covered in blood. One of the loose shots of the drughead had hit Donna in the temple and she was not moving. Mack got down to see how she was but he could see that her eyes were open and lifeless. It seemed to Mack that this was some sort of nightmare. How could Donna not be alive? Why wasn't he the one to be shot? His world had been broken apart in one minute flat and he couldn't take it in.

The paramedics had now arrived and they gently asked Mack to let them do their job. One of the policemen walked up to Mack "listen mate, I don't know what went on here but could you just give me some details and we will need you to come down the station to give us your side of things". Mack was in a daze. He looked at the paramedics tending to Donna, a couple more were crouched over the drug dealing monster that had ruined his life. Mack briefly wondered how he could have caused more suffering to the cunt but it was too late now.

Mack was led outside by one of the policemen and he was taken down the station.

He gave his statement as best he could recall and was released on bail pending further enquiries.

Clearly the CCTV would show events in the bar and that he had ended the life of the gunman.

An autopsy was ordered for Donna and the subsequent inquest delivered a verdict of unlawful killing. The CID and the CPS conducted and inquiry involving witnesses and video evidence. As the gunman had already fired his weapon before Mack got to him they ruled that he could only have acted in self-defence, the only question mark was of use of excessive force. Because of this they had no choice but to charge Mack with manslaughter and let the courts sort it out. Donna's body was released so that a funeral could be held. This was a small, personal service and Mack was on autopilot all day still really unable to accept she was gone. The thoughts were starting to form in his mind however, that this was the result of illegal thugs dealing in illegal substances using illegal weapons in an underworld that, up to now, he had had little awareness of. Apart from dealing with the smack dealers in the club a couple of years back, Mack had no need to mix in the scum world of class A drugs. The school bully had got what he deserved but surely he was simply a soldier in the Devil's army and there would be many more where he came from. The fact was, thought Mack, that A. the thug had spotted Mack and B. He was carrying a gun in public and was quite prepared to shoot Mack regardless of the consequences.

This fucker clearly lived in a world where this was

possible and he had no regard for another human life. Clearly this attitude applied to drug dealing, pimping, human trafficking, or any other illegal activity. He had developed his disregard of human life to such an extent that Mack's life was expendable, in fact forfeit for humiliating him in the pub that night. Mack had absolutely no regrets for taking the life of the scumbag. If he had any regrets it was only that the cunt might have died in pain of some complication at a later time. All these thought were spinning around Mack's mind. It was affecting his work and his social life and he had to try to make some sense of it all or he would become another victim of the evil doer, and that wasn't going to happen.

Two months later the trial started and evidence was heard, mainly from Mack's side. The video evidence was shown and the prosecution tried to propose that snapping the neck of the thug was 'excessive force'.

Mack's defence laid out his standing in the community, his previous good character and the extreme circumstances that the event had created, notwithstanding the death of Mack's fiancée.

The jury retired and took ten minutes to find Mack not guilty of manslaughter or any other offence for that matter. In fact the chairman of the jury took it upon himself to praise Mack's speed of action in preventing further bloodshed. The judge also praised Mack's actions whilst dismissing the case and apologising for the fact that he had to go through all this on top of all he had to deal with.

Mack was in limbo for months, simply bumbling along and going through the motions. His colleagues at work understood his pain and gave him as much space as possible. Ultimately though, everything Mack did and everything in his life reminded him of Donna. After some considerable thought he realized he had to get away. He put the house up for sale, said his farewells and jetted off to find some sort of peace and normality, if there could ever be such a thing for him.

At the time, moving to the Spanish coast seemed like the ideal thing. As we have seen he had had little experience of the seedier side of life. It probably wasn't the best choice to come to the Costa del Crime then but it would ultimately give him the purpose in life he needed so desperately.

CHAPTER 21

Buttershaw

Mack had returned to the UK for a few weeks to sort out the sale of his house and tie up some loose ends with Donna's estate and family. He was starting to have clearer thought as to how the world worked and how he intended to affect it in his way. Donna had been taken from him as a result of shitbags who thought they could live in a world apart from the rest of society and get away with it. Possibly a spell behind bars for them now and then but, nowadays, sentencing was getting so soft for drug offences it was hardly worth worrying about. Anyway, three meals a day and cable TV for a few months who would give a fuck? What they didn't know was Mack's deep burning hatred for these scum. They would never know, until it hit them, that there was a new type of justice and it would not involve a soft sentence and a social worker.

Mack needed to start pushing back against this evil. He decided to look up the skeleton in Buttershaw who had asked him for protection some time ago. This would be as good a place to start as any.

The Buttershaw council estate in Bradford had a deserved reputation as a deprived, rough estate where the rule of law had failed. Hardly anybody worked full-time - or anytime for that matter. Class A drug use was rife and there were no foot patrols by the police. The police attitude was that they sold drugs to each other, burgled each other's houses and stabbed and maimed each other. It would be impossible to clean up or establish any kind of law and order so they just paid lip-service to policing the district and only got involved if the trouble leaked out of the estate.

Now, this may be okay for lazy policing with limited resources, but not everyone on the estate was an evil drug peddling bastard. Some people had no option. Down on their luck they had been allocated housing in this stinking pit and had to try and survive. Mack knew this and would do what he could to take out whatever evil he could.

Mack called in the local pub asking after the scumbag. "What do you want to see him for?" asked a scruffy shitbag that Mack had approached. "It's not me that want him, it's him that wants me" said Mack. He gave the tosser his number and told him to arrange contact. He gave the scruffy twat a twenty pound note for his troubles. "Get yourself a drink, but don't let me down OK"

The skeleton called Mack on his mobile later that evening. "Hey up geezer, long time no see! Are you looking for a bit of work?" "Yeah" said Mack "I'm over from Spain for a bit, just looking for a bit of cash work ". "Spot on" said the waster, I'll give you a ring later, I've got a couple of things going on that will just suit you". The next morning the skeleton called Mack "my team are going to pick up some gear this aft. Go with them and see everything goes down ok alright?" "please" said Mack. "Please what?" said the scumbag. "Say please you cunt" said Mack. "Don't talk to me like one your toerags or we won't be friends ok?" "Oh, ok for fuck's sake, don't get a cob on. Please go with the lads, ok?" "Tell them to text me when they are setting off, I'll be there" Mack clicked off the phone without another word. It was going to be hard to deal with this motherfucker without filling him in at the first opportunity, but the chance of dealing him a severe blow, in more than the physical sense, was too good to spoil.

At 2 o'clock he got a text from one of the lackeys to meet at the end of a nearby avenue. Mack would simply follow in his own car and observe.

The gang turned up in an old Vauxhall Astra that clearly had not passed the MOT and was far from roadworthy Mack followed it for a mile down the road and pulled up a few yards away. Awaiting the gang were two dodgy looking individuals of Asian heritage (Bradford had more than its fair share of south Asian immigrants). Shaved heads, black tracksuits and Nike trainers, they were as obvious as if they had neon signs on the car saying "Heroin Dealer ". They were driving a late plate Audi S3 worth about thirty grand. It was incredible that these wankers were not stopped every hundred yards by the police and asked where they got the money from. Unfortunately the police knew the cunts would simply play the 'race' card' so they literally got away with murder. One of the Buttershaw gang got into the back of the car and money changed hands for a package. Mack took note of the number of the dealer's car; he had a mate in the CID who would get him an address.

Mack made sure the car returned to base and noted the property that the gang went into So far so good.

Bradford, in fact most of West Yorkshire, had areas of dense stone-built Victorian era housing that had been adopted by Bangladeshi/Pakistani immigrants and their descendants for decades. Arriving in the late fifties and early sixties to provide cheap night-shift labour for the woollen mills they were now no longer an ethnic minority. Bradford had in excess of 80,000 of its population of Asian heritage. Nowadays they were a self-supporting ghetto providing everything that was needed to live in a totally Asian environment from cradle to grave.

Most of them were concentrated around the now defunct Lister's Mill, formerly one of the largest mill complexes in the world. This included Manningham Lane and Oak Lane which now had become a stinking litter strewn shithole where no sensible ethnically white person would go.

They also had family connections with the heroin trade in Pakistan and Afghanistan. They imported huge amounts of legitimate goods from the sub-continent which made it all but impossible to stem the tide of class A product hidden in the con-signments flooding into the country.

Mack knew he could only give the Asians a poke in the eye as far as their illegal dealings were con-cerned but he would get some satisfaction from upsetting their little world in his own way. His target was the bottom feeders on the Buttershaw estate. Their removal would create a vacuum which would upset the local drug trade for some time.

The next day Mack got another call from the skel-eton. "Hey man, thanks for looking out for us yes-terday. I've got another little job this aft. Can you come round to mine about one?" "Don't know where you live" said Mack. The skeleton gave him the address. This gave Mack a small tingle. He was getting inside the inner circle. Happy days; not for them of course.

CHAPTER 22

Suit you sir?

Mack always presented himself well. At work he wore quality designer suits, fine cotton shirts and the best shoes. Actually his shoes were the most important to him. Unusually for a sporty type he didn't like trainers except for jogging and gym work. In the *dojo* he had always trained barefoot whatever the temperature. So, it didn't matter if he was wearing jeans or trousers, he had quality footwear.

The county of Northamptonshire was still the centre of excellence for British leather shoes. Mack liked Loakes Bros or Crockett and Jones. You couldn't beat a quality British brogue. Although he had now discovered the quality of Spanish footwear and would treat himself to a pair soon.

Mack had found, to his cost, that if you kicked someone in the skull, elbow or knee in bare feet you had better get your technique right. The front kick *mae geri* was produce by raising the knee almost to chest height and then extending the foot forward whilst at the same time thrusting the hip at the same time for maximum impact. The strike was made with the ball of the foot which was capable of delivering a devastating blow. When directed to the solar plexus, the chin or the groin with sufficient force it was usually all that was required.

The side and roundhouse kicks however were different. The side kick *yoko geri* was produced by turning to the side whilst drawing the knee almost to chest height then thrusting sideways into the body or head. The strike was with the back part of the foot, the side of the heel so the foot had to be turned slightly inward. This kick was most effective when moving forwards at the same time which delivered body weight as well as strength.

The roundhouse kick *mawashi geri* was delivered from the ground by drawing the knee out to the side and then extending the leg and striking with the ball of the foot by flexing the foot forwards. This was difficult to achieve and many students, wearing foot pads, would use the top of the foot. In the *dojo* they were not using any force anyway. If you tried this with any force at all, especially if blocked with the hand or elbow, you could easily break a metatarsal. It was the same with hand strikes; you very rarely used the open hand or you could break your fingers. The fist was the way to go.

The beauty of really good shoes therefore was that, when you delivered these kicks, you didn't need to worry about the ball of the foot or the heel or the metatarsals. A hand stitched leather sole or a steel lined leather heel would do nicely thank you. A smashed jawbone with several teeth removed was often the result of Mack's kicks. He didn't need to worry about bending his toes back, in fact technique went out of the window, just stoved your foot into the fucker's head, any part would do but Mack was surgically accurate.

It wasn't quite cheating; actually Mack's shoes were fucking expensive but you had to get value for money didn't you?

CHAPTER 23

Gerald Chippendale

It was the most unfortunate event if you lived on a sink estate to be named after your grandad. He would have loved to be called Wayne or Michael. Yeah, Michael or Mick or Micky that would have helped but no; Gerald it was. So Gerald had become Gez or Jez as soon as possible. Anyone who found out his name was Gerald and used it to take the piss soon regretted it. And if that wasn't bad enough; he had the surname of a famous troupe of half-naked male dancers who were popular with the ladies. Nobody on his estate knew there was a famous furniture maker of the same name. The world where that furniture was still to be found was a universe away from Buttershaw. So acquaintances who knew him well enough would refer to him as Jez Chip and that avoided any retribution from the vicious little fucker.

In low life land you didn't always need to be the biggest to be the 'hardest'. Being 'hard' in this world was measured by either how tough you were in a fist fight (or knife fight or iron bar fight or any other type of fight) or was also measured in deficiency of moral fibre. The level of viciousness, the tendency to use a weapon, the habit of going too far in administering injury. Size didn't always matter; nastiness did.

Jez hardly went to school, junior or senior. He preferred hanging around town in the coffee shops. Even in his pre-teens he was a skilled thief, shoplifter and bag snatcher. He had learned at an unbelievably early age that the authorities could do absolutely nothing to stop him. The soppy twats who had studied Sociology at 'Uni' thought they could get him to change by talking to him. He used to tell his pals what they used to try whilst laughing like a drain.

If he had his collar felt by the local constabulary he would call them cunts and wankers, he would kick and scream and he would tell everyone who tried to engage with him to fuck off. They had no powers of arrest with an eight year old, they could do nothing; nothing whatsoever.

His mum didn't give a fuck. She was a smack head who actually sent him out to nick stuff to sell to feed her habit. She didn't pay rent or Council Tax; in fact she contributed nothing to society except being a burden and a cost.

As Jez grew into his teens he lost the legal protection of being a minor and had already spent a couple of short spells in a detention centre. Again, this was utterly pointless. The only thing detention gave young Jez was three meals a day and a criminal education.

Jez moved from petty theft to drug dealing easily. After all, his mum was a smack head and she would usually send him out to score for her. He got to know the pusher and soon agreed to helping out in distributing his wares. Being a 'runner' helped Jez to learn the ropes. He learned that the users didn't always pay up front. It could be useful for the dealers to allow someone to run up a debt. By way of payment they would then use the addict's home as a drug den or 'cuckoo's nest'. Other users who didn't pay would be encouraged to do so by a severe beating and confiscation of anything of value that they possessed. Jez liked dishing it out; it made him feel important.

Jez's mum died of liver failure aged thirty four. She contracted hepatitis C some years ago and had been told that continued heroin use would lead to an early death. If that wasn't incentive enough to seek help what was? But such was the grip of the drug coupled with the weakness of character of Jez's mum that she simply killed herself slowly.

Jez took over the non-payment of rent or Council Tax on the property and continued to add to the deterioration both inside and out.

It is an immutable fact that the life of a heroin dealer is not a long one. And so it was that the pusher that Jez worked for decided to try and rip off the Asian gang that supplied him. He had told them that some people owed him money and could he pay them in a couple of days. They had agreed and he had sold the whole consignment to the gang across Halifax Road on the Woodside estate. He was the wrong person to hold a bundle of cash and had gone out and bought the latest iPhone and a stolen scooter.

When the Asians came calling he had waffled and spluttered and lied but ultimately he had blown the cash; he was fucked.

Mohammed Raffiq, one of the Asian gang, got in touch with Jez and explained to him that his pusher had left the area and wouldn't be coming back and would he like to take on the business? No brainer really, this was Jez's destiny, to be the main pusher in Buttershaw. It was a huge estate and there were plenty of potential victims, of course he would. The Asians extended Jez a line of credit which he managed meticulously. He wasn't educated but he wasn't stupid either. His pusher hadn't 'left the area' he knew full well what had happened to him and he would make sure that he didn't follow in his footsteps. Besides he was a respectable businessman now or whatever that meant in Jez's world.

Jez had built the business and had found other low life wankers to do his dirty work. Jez paid well and had settled into the life of a hard drug pusher with relish. He also looked at opportunities to expand his operation and had heard that the Northern Soul scene was ripe with drug users. Mostly this was amphetamine and E's to help them dance a lot but Jez suggested to his boys that they try to move a bit of the harder stuff. One day his boys came back from the casualty department of Bradford Royal Infirmary looking in a right state. They had been sorted out properly. This wasn't in the script and there had been a couple of users that had been developed at the Northern Soul club. Whoever had done this to his boys must be one seriously hard fucker. The lads had told him it had been just one bloke. Jesus, it looked as if they had been hit by a train.

Now, we already know that if you are 'hard' you must be a criminal type no? So Jez decided to see if this individual could be paid/bribed or otherwise encouraged to come on board and earn some good money. Money talks – right?

CHAPTER 24

Mohammed Raffiq

Mohammad, Mahommad, Mahommed in all its versions this was the most popular boys name in the UK and yet they were still referred to as an ethnic minority. When were the soppy twats going to wake up? There were over 80,000 Asian heritage inhabitants of Bradford and similar representations in Birmingham, London, Bolton, Blackburn, Glasgow and so on. Ethnic minority? Bollocks.

Mohammed was typical of his ilk; he was born in Bradford but considered himself British Asian or better still Pakistani. Funny that, they wanted to be Pakistanis but never wanted to live there. Anyway rant over.

Mohammed Raffiq was what he was for better or worse; it's too late now to do anything about it. He lived in a terrace house off Carlisle Road with his mum and dad and grandmother, two sisters and three brothers. These were large houses of the Victorian era built to house the workers in the woollen mills. Just round the corner was the massive Lister's Mill once one of the largest worsted spinning mills in the country. Now, in common with many others, it was a business park housing dozens of small and large businesses that occupied workshops and offices. Back in the fifties and sixties Mohammed's predecessors had been actively encouraged to leave their homeland and come and do the work that the increasingly affluent native population no longer wanted to do; tending the looms on day and night shifts. What they couldn't foresee was the decline in the industry through increasing overheads and competition from the East. Actually the daft thing was that the looms were bought and relocated to the countries that the immigrant workers had come from. Ironic or what?

Mohammed's parents had wanted him to go to University which in Bradford meant attending the local ex polytechnic which had been renamed Bradford University. It had neither a good reputation nor any standing in the academic world. An average grade Degree from Bradford Uni was about as much use as a chocolate fireguard. Most of the alumni ended up working in banks and insurance companies of which there were several large ones in Bradford.

Mohammed had passed on this questionable opportunity and had ended up as a waiter in one of the seemingly hundreds of curry houses in Bradford. Rightly rated as the curry capital of the UK you could choose the quality and cost of your curry from a few quid to a banquet in one of the modern glass palaces such as Akhbar's or Aagrah. He was not on his own; literally thousands of Asians worked in the catering industry in Bradford. It was either that or drive a taxi; or both.

In common with many of his 'brothers' he had a low opinion of the indigenous white population regarding them as privileged as well as *kuffar* (non-believers). Nowadays there were several large mosques in Bradford and you could regularly hear the *Adhan* or call to prayer by the *muezzin* although these days it was usually just a recording played through loudspeakers; that's progress for you.

The dislike of the white *kuffar* was intensified by the fact that they often chose to call for a curry on their way home from quaffing about a gallon of the devil's brew down the pub. Loud and obnoxious he had to tolerate being called 'Jimmy' by the drunken mob. "Oy Jimmy, two lamb bhunas and a garlic naan quick as you can!" he fucking hated them.

So he had no problem in jumping at the opportunity to help a 'brother' who had a nice little number providing heroin to a slum estate on the way to Halifax. It pleased him that he was dealing in misery. As opposed to his white counterparts who simply had no morals; Mohammed revelled in the fact that he was doing the infidels harm. The 'brother' used a small terrace house around the corner from Mohammed's home and he would help weigh and bag up the fixes. He had accompanied his friend a couple of times in making the drops. The last time he had noticed a car parked across the road observing proceedings but taking no part in the operation. This was a nice little side-line for Mohammed; he supplemented his meagre wage from the curry house and could afford the nicer models of mobile phone. Yeah, life was sweet.

CHAPTER 25

"Are you fucking mad?"

Buttershaw in winter was the most miserable shithole you could imagine. Hardly anybody tended their gardens, they were usually just places to put half-finished projects; cars on axle stands, scooters with no engines, old beds and sofas. There was an all pervading smell of decay and old sweat as well as a general air of despondency.

Mack now knew where the skeleton lived. He also knew where the Asians lived. The Asians were a drop in the ocean and he could not stem the tide of human despair being imported from the subcontinent. He would, however, put these particular fuckers out of circulation for some considerable time (at least). The skeleton would be more of a success as he was a main supplier on the estate. Perhaps, just perhaps, the addicts would be forced to seek out methadone fixes and come under the umbrella of the support services. That was possibly a naive hope but stemming the flow of badly cut heroin must have some beneficial effect. Firstly Mack needed to know when the next shipment was due. This part was easy as he was running protection for the lackeys. Thursday of that week Mack received the call he had been waiting for. The skeleton was on the phone, "Hiya pal, I've got some gear coming this aft, can you look after the lads....please. They'll text you for the meet later OK?" "No problem" said Mack and clicked off. This put the wheels in motion.

Mack had been provided an address off Carlisle Road smack bang in the middle of what might as well be in the Punjab. There was no evidence that native English people lived here and had not done so for a very long time. The loony left politicians crowed on about multi ethnic societies, cultural identities, and multiculturalism. There was no such thing. There was only one culture here, one religion which was drilled into them from cradle to grave, more than one language but none of them English. There were more takeaways than anybody could ever make profit from, but that was irrelevant. They were only there to clean money. There were used car lots dealing in exotic cars; high end German and Italian metal that clearly no local could afford. It was so obviously crooked it was laughable, but nobody did anything about it for fear of being branded 'racist'.

Mack parked on Oak Lane and walked a couple of hundred yards to a stone built terraced street. There were BMW's, Mercedes and Audis all over the place. Parked on double yellow lines, on corners in fact, anywhere they fucking liked.

Appropriately number 13 was his destination, and their luck was not in.

Asians traditionally did not lock their doors; they interacted a lot with relatives and neighbours and liked easy access. Mack pulled his favourite tool from his sleeve. The thick end of a split pool cue, about three feet long and tapered and made from very hard wood. He walked in the gate and straight into the house. These houses did not have entrance hallways, he was straight into the living room where three shaven headed scum were bagging up white powder. "What the fuck!" exclaimed one of the filthy wankers. Mack didn't hesitate he smashed the nearest one round the head with the cue and that was the end of him. The others jumped back putting some distance between themselves and Mack. The speed he could move at made it irrelevant. One of them had pulled out a mobile phone and the other one had pulled a knife. With lightning precision he broke the forearm of the fucker with the knife, instantly turning to pummel the face of the other to a bloody mess. The arsehole with the knife had now turned to blubbering, "what do you want man? I can give you money innit!"

The word 'innit' had become synonymous with the Asian accent. They now had so little interaction with traditional British or Yorkshire society that they had regressed generationally from at least some integration. Where many of their parents had traditional northern accents, these twats had a strange mixture of Asian and gangster accents. Anyway, do you think Mack wanted any money from this leech? Mack didn't even break stride he stoved the cue into the shithead's face and then destroyed his skull with a massive blow to the back of his head. Whether he lived or died made no difference to Mack when the red mist descended. If he lived he would be a cabbage or a cripple or both, so fucking what. There had been surprisingly little commotion during the attack. It was so fast, so severe they had no time to scream and it was over in seconds. Mack took stock of his situation. The table in the room was covered in something illegal, cocaine or speed or something of that ilk. Mack checked the cupboards downstairs and up and found what he was looking for. Stacks of cash in used notes. Thousands of pounds. Pulling out a nylon sack he filled it with all he could find. He then went into the kitchen and turned on all the gas burners. Checking the drawers he found a candle and set it in the corner of the kitchen, lighting it and letting himself out of the back door. A woman across the alley dressed like she lived in Bangladesh noticed him then looked away. People were always coming and going from that house. As he returned to his car he heard a distant 'whoomph'. One down, one to go.

Mack returned to Buttershaw to await the text. About one o'clock it came and he replied "change of plan, meet me at Jez's house" Jez being the name of the skeleton. Mack then set off for the scum-bag's house and approached with his cue butt up his sleeve. Two minutes later the beat up old car pulled up with the three tossers in it. Mack nodded at the three and motioned for them to go into the house and he followed them in. Jez was in the front room with another of his crony's bagging up deal sized portions of cocaine. Looking up he saw the three who were supposed to be on their way to the pick-up and Mack who was supposed to be looking out for them. "What's this?" asked the skeleton looking bemused. "End of the road for you" replied Mack pulling out the cue. "Are you fucking mad?" was what he meant to say but all he got out was "are you fuck.." before the cue smashed him in the face. As was mentioned before, he only needed a blue tooth for a snooker set; his dental problems were over now. The skeleton went down clutching his face while Mack set about the rest of them who were falling over each other trying to get out of the way. Skulls, arms, hands and legs were broken as Mack let them have everything they were entitled to. Mack picked up the groaning skeleton by his collar, the fear in his eyes palpable. "You are a stain on the underpants of life" grizzled Mack as he dropped the mother-fucker and laid into him with royal vengeance.

He then went through the house bagging up all the cash he could find. One thing he did find was a loaded Berretta pistol beside the stinking bed. This was why he had needed to strike quickly and with extreme violence, you couldn't trust these fuckers with any reaction time. Get in first, get in hard, make it count.

He then took a lighter from the pocket of one of the lackeys. They never worked and always smoked, funny that. Holding it to the downstairs curtain until the flames caught he walked out and across the estate to his car. He wouldn't be back in Buttershaw - ever.

Driving down the Halifax road towards Odsal stadium, home of the Bradford Bulls, Mack reflected on his day's work. He was strangely calm as to the fate of these scumbags. They had no right to a normal existence whilst dishing out misery and violence as they did. Mack's mind was finding a path, a way forward. He had always been exceptionally gifted in the martial arts. He had learned how to use these in the real world. He would now use them to special effect; redressing the balance between good and evil. Yes, wherever Mack would find an opportunity to take some of these fuckers out of the picture he would do that. And he wouldn't lose a wink of sleep.

CHAPTER 26

Poco a poco

Fuengirola is a tourist resort on the Costa del Sol. One of the larger of the coastal resorts it has 7 Km of seafront adjacent to a man-made beach. The sand is imported and does not have the fine consistency of natural beach sand which would have been ground down over thousands of years. Nevertheless, it was a long and popular beach with the *paseo maritimo* running its entire length. Local Brits sometimes called it 'Funky Town' or 'Finger in yer Ola'.

The promenade was popular with skaters, cyclists and joggers and for most of it's length had a dedicated track away from the road. Mack made use of it for regular exercise and to gather his thoughts. He found it really therapeutic running along with his air-pods playing some classic Northern Soul, the beat was perfect for jogging and it took an effort of will to stop himself throwing a little jig or move whilst he was jogging along. At the far eastern end of the promenade was a roundabout which was simply a place to turn round and run back. He usually stopped at the Oasis bar for a *agua con gas* (sparkling water) before setting off back to the starting point. Sometimes he would run the other way towards the *Castillo Suel* a Moorish fort at the southern end of the promenade. In recent years a modern cable-stayed bridge had given access to the full length of the *paseo* and you could run right past the old Roman fish salting factory.

The Mediterranean was a shimmering still pond. In Fuengirola the current driven up from the Atlantic stirred the sea so that it was not the clear subtropical snorkel friendly water that you found further up the coast. Plus it was surprisingly cool. In fact it was quite murky and Mack preferred the local municipal swimming pool for pleasure swimming.

Alongside the *paseo* was bar after bar, restaurants, a few shops and multi-story apartment blocks. During the summer months most of the apartments were occupied with Spanish nationals using their second homes but from October to May the window shutters were pulled down and the properties were left empty.

The population of Fuengirola varied considerably, from 80,000 in the winter to over 250,000 in summer.

Once you went one street back from the front you found more bars and restaurants and further inland were even more. The unusual fact was, the further away from the seafront the bar was the more likely it was to survive. These smaller out-of-the-way bars had a more regular local trade, both Spanish and ex-pat; residents that lived and worked all year round keeping the wheels of the town turning. On the seafront all you could rely on was the tourists and tourists would not go into an empty bar and there were lots of those. It was amazing how many suckers there were who thought they could come to the Costa and make it in a seafront bar. It usually took them six months to spend all their hard earned savings before they slunk back to their country of origin, usually the UK. You could spot them a mile off, stood at the front of the terrace looking up and down the seafront to if there was anyone about and wonder why they weren't coming into their bar/café. Week in week out throwing food away and watching barrels of beer go off. You could almost feel sorry for them but the problem was that none of them had done any homework or observation before taking the plunge. And word would not get around back home that the Costa del Sol was a shit place to buy a bar because they would not tell anybody how stupid they had been.

Mack lived out of the way in a back street of mostly Spanish residents. It may seem strange pointing out that they were mostly Spanish residents in a Spanish town in Spain but it was perfectly possible, in this part of the world, to live a completely British life in a British complex with British bars reading British newspapers and watching British TV (same for Germans or Scandinavians). And being typically lazy, the Brits used this as an excuse to speak no Spanish whatsoever. In a town like Fuengirola this was all too easy to do. All the bars and restaurants relied on foreign visitors and had English speaking staff. Typically English was also used by visiting (or resident) Germans, Scandinavians and other nationalities in order to be understood.

Mack was not of the same mind. First of all he didn't want to be among the typically British residents. To him they were brash and ignorant. Plus he didn't really want to be seen among them. He knew the *Policia Nacional* had plain clothes officers hanging around various bars secretly noting local activities. They knew who was working legitimately and who had undeclared or unexplained income. They had access to all the systems necessary to investigate a person's background.

For the most part the *Policia Nacional* had enough on their plates with illegal Spanish and Moroccan activity but they were not ignorant of the fact that the Moroccans had contacts in the Brit underworld and were distributing various illegal drugs. One of Mack's favourite bars was the 'Majesty' situated a couple of streets back and frequented by more mature Brits and Scandinavians with none of the typical loudmouth Brits who, for some reason seemed to always come from the south of the UK and were potty mouthed arseholes. Mack actually wanted to learn Spanish as best he could and had bought a few self-help books and tried, where he could, to converse with local Spanish residents. Sometimes it worked sometimes it didn't but, as the Spanish told him, you have to learn *poco a poco* - little by little.

Mack had bought his apartment following the sale of his UK house. After paying the mortgage off he had enough equity to buy a small two bed two bathroom apartment which was quite well appointed. He had marble floors and quality bathroom fittings. The en-suite had a walk-in shower and the kitchen had all the modern appliances including a dishwasher. From his lounge he had a small balcony, big enough for a plastic table and chairs where he could chill and top up his tan with a nice glass of *rioja*.

There were still bargains to be had on the coast but they were getting fewer by the minute. He went many places by scooter and found this ideal to explore the backstreets and seldom visited areas of the town. The maximum engine he could use on his car licence was 125cc but he had bought a tuning chip to add a bit more power and it was actually pretty nippy.

Once a year Fuengirola celebrated the *Feria de los Pueblos* at the fairground; a facility which many larger towns had. The city of Málaga had the largest annual traditional feria in Spain but this one in Fuengirola was an additional annual gathering celebrating the international nature of the town and the traditional Spanish casitas (dedicated buildings used for various clubs and associations in the town) were turned over to representatives of different countries and the other regions of Spain to provide authentic food, dress, music and alcoholic beverages pertinent to the culture of that community. There were fairground rides and shops but the main activity was touring the various bars and sampling the different drinks available. Mack was out with his girlfriend Jill, who had witnessed him dealing with Big Phil and knew he trained with Martin but generally had no idea of how violent Mack could be when the red mist descended (and he didn't want her to either)

The thing was, Mack did not lose control when dealing with drug dealing wankers, he simply had such a deep seated hate that they became as nothing. He didn't care how badly he injured them or if they didn't survive the encounter. They had made a life choice and the consequences were that they ran the risk of violent encounters. The problem for the low-life scum was that they generally expected the violence to be either instigated by themselves or in retaliation for some transgression by a rival gang. They never expected that the violence would come from this mild mannered Yorkshire bloke, or that it would be so devastating.

The incident in Bradford that had robbed him of

Donna had affected Mack so badly that he saw it as his mission in life to make these fuckers suffer. They peddled misery and despair and laughed about it. They had no concern that the victims of their trade would steal from family members and friends to fund their habit. The misery extended beyond the direct recipient of the drugs; it affected communities, families, marriages and relationships beyond measure.

Often the cunts considered themselves untouchable. They lived in a world where threats and violent actions engendered fear and they loved the elevated position that fear gave them. The bosses surrounded themselves with lackeys and sycophants who fed on the free drinks and generally elevated status their association gave them. They liked to intimidate and to threaten, especially members of the general public who, they knew, would never raise a finger to them. It was this attitude that riled Mack so much. His hatred was so intense it he had to physically push it to the back of his mind to live an outwardly normal life and enjoy normality with a few normal people.

And so it was that his small group had a policy of 'last man standing' when it came to the annual event. During the evening they visited Argentina, Brazil, Peru, Asturias and many, many more before wobbling home individually to wake up slightly regretful and worse for wear. Mack was grateful that there were people in his life that kept him grounded and gave him a place to come back to when he had 'taken care of business'.

CHAPTER 27

"This ends here"

Following his dealings with the Ukrainians Mack had a bag full of cash and a bag full of Class A heroin and the last thing he needed was to be stopped by the Guardia Civil. So he was driving steadily up the A7 to Puerto Bánus having achieved half of what he had set out to do this morning. There would be a large police investigation in Estepona about to get underway and he needed to be off the road ASAP.

Driving past Benavista into Gualdalmina he cruised through San Pedro Alcántara before turning off to Puerto Banús. He parked in the underground carpark in the centre of the urban development and tucked the car away in a corner. The car would have to go, which was a shame; he liked the BMW. After he was finished here he was confident he could make a nice cash purchase for his next car.

He knew he would need to be quick, unannounced and vicious. He had no idea if word could have reached Handforth. He doubted it would have done as any police presence in Estepona would put off any other associates of the Ukrainians and they would not have a full picture of what had gone on plus, as far as he knew, nobody down there knew how to contact Handforth. The portly man and his fat wife may have seen him briefly but they were sat in the back of a police car contemplating their ruined holiday.

Mack took his trusty pool cue from the car and didn't really bother concealing it, he just held it behind his back. He walked up the stairs out of the carpark, into the sunshine and headed for Handforth's den.

As he walked into the room he knew he hadn't been rumbled by the grin on the Neanderthal's face. "Mack my boy! What a pleasant sight you are! Where's the bag?" This was typical of this type of scum. No concern as to how the deal had gone down or whether there had been anything to report, no; all he was interested in was the money.

As usual Handforth was attended by Skeletor and Buster Bloodvessel despite their useless performance the last time that Mack had encountered them. They would be no more useful now.

"The bag is in the car with the gear. I'm keeping the money and chucking the drugs, this ends here". Handforth was momentarily confused, trying to process this news. Momentarily was all Mack needed. He smashed Skeletor round the head with the cue instantly knocking him out. He immediately launched a side kick to the head of the fat one rendering him confused enough to not see the cue driving into the back of his skull and crushing the bone into his brain. Two down. Bear in mind that, even though Handforth was witnessing this, it was a case of 'smash' 'kick' 'smash' in the time it takes you to read the words. Reaction time was miniscule plus, he was a fat useless cunt who hadn't raised a hand in anger for years. He was, however, not the local kingpin for nothing. He stood up, at the same time launching the desk with enormous strength. "Come on then you cunt, I'll fucking kill yer!" and he probably thought he would; if he could get to Mack and get hold of him. "Mack was cool as a cucumber; he launched a powerful straight side kick to the thug's head spinning him backwards. He then did it again, and again. The fat bastard had a strong neck and was powerfully built under the layers of podge. However, when you are kicked with the power that Mack could generate, you are on a hiding to nothing. Mack waded in with punches to the head, he then drove his fingers into the eye sockets of the fat mess destroying his vision, probably forever (which wouldn't be long). Taking the cue and holding it by the thin end he rained blow after blow on the head of the drug dealing scumbag until the head was unrecognisable as such. He then did the same to the other two evil fuckers. All he could think of whilst raining vicious blows on these filthy low-life scum was Donna lying on the floor of the pub with her unseeing eyes. It didn't matter that these fuckers had nothing to do with Donna's death; they were all the same to Mack.

He then picked the safe keys off the floor and opened it. There were tens of thousands of euros in neat stacks. Mack filled a bag and headed out. He hadn't been there above two minutes and there had been surprisingly little commotion. Mack had considered setting fire to the place but he didn't need the added attention to come too soon. It could be days before the carnage was discovered; as opposed to Estepona where the police were trying to piece together what and who they were dealing with. Before too long they would realize what the Ukrainians were up to and come to the conclusion that someone had done them a big favour. The lead investigator would write up his report and file it under gang related violence. He wouldn't waste any more time investigating a crime that he didn't personally believe was a crime anyway. They had enough on their plate with living drug dealing arseholes without worrying about dead ones.

He returned to his car and put the bag of cash with the rest of the money and the bag of heroin. He drove the car out of the carpark. The car park was one of the few places with public CCTV and he didn't want to be seen carrying the bags out of the carpark. He drove around the corner; at two thirty in the afternoon most Spanish towns were deserted for 'siesta', he still couldn't get his head round the afternoon shut-down between two and five o'clock. Mack parked the car on a zebra crossing and walked off. Within half an hour it would be towed away by the municipal *grua* (tow truck). One thing the Spanish were incredibly efficient at was keeping the streets clear. They were that good you could literally pop in a shop for a newspaper and come out and find your car gone. The car would be taken to the *deposito municipal* - compound. There it would stay until the parking fine and recovery was paid for. After a length of time without payment it would be scrapped. You can't register a car in Spain without all the necessary paperwork especially from the previous owner. Without the paperwork the car is useless so they couldn't sell the car to be used on Spanish roads. Furthermore he would deregister the car with a local *gestoria* (public administrator) making sure that the fine would not end up with him. He would also report the car stolen to the local police. No doubt the police would report back to him that the car had been found in Puerto Banús; but with the registration cancelled Mack wouldn't need to worry about it.

He then headed for the harbour of Puerto Banús carrying his rucksack and a holdall. There is a huge man-made sea wall protecting the harbour from the Mediterranean and Mack walked casually along it. A couple of other tourists were strolling along the wall too so Mack sat down on the edge and looked out to sea contemplating his day's work .From here you could often see the rock of Gibraltar and very occasionally, weather conditions permitting, the coast of North Africa. Behind him were row upon row of luxury yachts and motor cruisers. Hundreds of millions of pounds of hardware with a mixture of legitimate owners and wankers who were bent as a butcher's hook. Either into white collar crime such as timeshare scams or into more dodgy matters such as Mack may be concerned with.

Lee Handforth had been a low-life scumbag before he had come to the Costa del Sol, he was so evil he had to leave Manchester to avoid being seen off by rival evil motherfuckers. He had established contacts and connections on the coast that had allowed him to live the life of Reilly from his ill-gotten gains. He peddled poison, misery and violence to people whose life had taken a wrong turn. He wallowed in his position as kingpin and his aura of intimidation. He had absolutely zero consideration of the results of his actions; he just wanted more and more money.

The Ukrainians were equally nasty evil fuckers before they came to the Costa del Sol. Their home environment was challenging due to the upheaval following the break-up of the USSR. Criminal gangs reigned unopposed and territory was fought over viciously. Without oil none of the former Soviet Republics had large industries or thriving economies. The ones that did were riddled with corruption. So unemployment was high and desperation equally so. This had led to a breeding ground for violent evil fuckers hell bent on making money anyway they could.

This particular bunch of evil fuckers had heard of the rich picking to be had in the south of Spain and had sought out an area with little competition. They wanted to operate unopposed. At least if anyone did oppose them they would find out how evil these scumbag Ukrainians could be. Guns, knives, whatever it took.

Now, following Mack's intervention, there would be a short period, a vacuum in which it would be safe to go about your daily business without being accused of 'looking' at someone the wrong way. The addicts would have to work a bit harder for their gear. It might be a bit more expensive and it might be a bit harder to come by. Hopefully, just hopefully, some of them may look for a way out.

Mack looked around and the walkway was clear. He launched the bag of heroin into the sea. It would be battered against the rocks and destroyed. No chance of anyone else getting hold of it although the fish might be spaced out for a while.

This had been a major blow against the criminal infrastructure on the coast. As far as Mack was aware, his involvement would not be noticed. He had had little contact with the Ukrainians, his name would not be local knowledge. Handforth had kept Mack's involvement to himself. Only the security manager at the night club had any knowledge that Mack was in contact with Handforth. He was sure he was under the radar. He would hope to keep it that way. Mack walked back to the centre of the port and climbed into a waiting taxi. "Fuengirola por favor" he asked the driver. This would be a good fare for the driver. *Bueno*.

CHAPTER 28

Mujahid

Mujahid El Haloui smoked a 'Ducados' cigarette, a popular Spanish brand similar to a Gitane made with dark aromatic tobacco. He lounged on a sofa in a scruffy apartment in the Carvajal district of Fuengirola. Fuengirola had four distinct *barrios* or suburbs. Fuengirola, Los Boliches, Torreblanca with Carvajal being the most easterly and nearest to Benalmádena. Carvajal was the least commercial area of Fuengirola with few hotels, less bars and quieter beaches. The Moroccan gang rented an apartment from another Moroccan for a ridiculous rent. The problem was; no-one would rent an apartment to young Moroccans so they had limited choice. The rent wasn't a problem as they had a tasty little business going on dealing marijuana, MDMA and ketamine around the clubs and bars in the town. They had recently branched out into dealing heroin and had found the profit margins were very lucrative.

The leader of this little group of filth was Hadir Kaghat, a particularly nasty scumbag. Shaven headed and with a permanent seven o'clock shadow, he was a typical soap dodging drug dealing ne'er do well whose only aim was to sell any type or quality of illegal substance to absolutely anyone regardless of the effect or outcome. He considered himself a proper gangster. He always carried a blade and would use it either for effect or for dishing out injury or worse, He enjoyed seeing *kuffar* bleeding, they meant nothing to him.

His hand was still bandaged after having his blade pushed through it by the English bastard at the Heaven's Door nightclub. He was seething with hate and rage, the English infidel had told him what he would do if he was seen again around the club; well Hadir Kaghat would show this white honkey fucker what he was made of.

He was sat at the dining table of his shitty little hovel to give him a higher seating level so he looked more important. He was planning revenge for the humiliation he had suffered at the hands of this non-believer, he would take his team and end his life; he would slice him and dice him and make him suffer before finishing him off by beheading him. Yes, this was God's will; nothing could resist his crew when they went in tooled up and ready for action.

Planning this act of *jihad* were three other scruffy Moroccan wankers as well as Mujahid. Abdelhamid Diouri, Jaul Jouiti and Wasim Seddiki had all grown up in a slum area of Tangiers. And when you talk of slums in Tangiers, they are not like slums in British towns and cities which are palaces by comparison, no; this was depravity on an inhuman scale. No running water or electricity, obviously no TV's laptops, mobile phones, fridges or any of the trappings of modern Europe. This was the dark ages and when they had the opportunity to sneak aboard a ferry to Algeciras in the back of a lorry load of leather jackets they had literally jumped at the chance.

During the summer months it was easy to sleep rough on the Costa del Sol. It hardly rained and night time temperatures allowed a person to bed down anywhere out of sight of the police who would arrest you for vagrancy. As they were illegal immigrants they needed to avoid any contact with the police. If you were caught in Spain they didn't mess about or consider your 'human rights' they simply sent you back where you came from. They stole food and clothing and manged to sell a few mobile phones stolen from unwary tourists to keep them in cigarettes.

They made their way up the coast to Fuengirola which was the busiest resort and had the richest pickings. They became experts at shoplifting and spiriting mobile phone away from idiots who just left them on tables. There was no point looking for normal work, they had no skills or experience, not one of them had ever worked a day for wages plus, they were illegal immigrants so couldn't be registered for work anyway. Not that any of this mattered and they had no option but to live on their wits and pilfer anything they could. In any case this was ten times better than Morocco even with nowhere to live. There were enough unfinished buildings to bed down in and even unfinished buildings were a step up for them. They were literally as thick as thieves.

Eventually they bumped into Hadir; it was easy to spot other Moroccans as they were all soap dodging smelly fuckers with buzz cuts and cheap knock-off clothes. Hadir introduced them to the drug dealers and soon they were peddling their filth; initially as pushers for other dealers and inevitably establishing their own little business and finding accommodation. They couldn't believe it when they had acquired enough money to afford their own flat. Life was sweet for the gang. They had laptops, a TV with Moroccan channels, mobile phones and refrigerated food. Fuck me this was luxury, they had dreams of moving up the ladder and becoming big time gangsters, they talked about what they would buy and the houses they would live in just as Europeans talked about what they would do if they won the Lottery. Remember, they couldn't buy a lottery ticket, they were illegals.

Hadir was engaging the gang and discussing how they would attack the nightclub and establish their authority in Fuengirola. This would be a major move for the group; with such a move they would be seen as proper gangsters and enforcers. They would have all the respect and kudos and would be able to establish a wider territory. This was to be their big step; sort the English bastard out and let it be known among the criminal fraternity who had carried out the execution. Their stomachs were churning with anticipation; they were all a bundle of nerves. The reality was coming home to them but they would not falter. Now was their moment, no longer just bunch of scruffy cunts from the slums of Tangiers but like a board of directors with a business to run – not that they actually knew what a board of directors was.

To Hadir this would be straight forward. They knew what time the club closed and that the *kafir* was always last to leave. They would storm the club, kill the infidel and anyone else who got in their way. Armed with two 18" machetes and three 'zombie' knives they would inflict maximum carnage and leave it like a scene from a horror movie. They had just discovered horror movies and they were their favourite entertainment. Tonight was the night and Hadir would have said a prayer if he knew any. He didn't attend the mosque and neither did the others. They considered themselves Muslim and *mujahedeen;* this would be a righteous kill *inshallah* and Allah would be proud of them. Actually, they had no idea if Allah would be proud of them but they told themselves that and it seemed to justify their plans.

They smoked until early morning talking about their luck in escaping the slums of Morocco and how their lives would change after tonight. They laughed to think how their reputation would improve. After tonight they would be real gangsters, in fact they may have to think of a name for their crew. Other filthy fuckers would be wanting to join them and they would be the bosses, dishing out the orders and having people working for *them.*

About three o'clock in the morning they left their stinking hole and swaggered their way west across town with their game faces on. This was their moment, their lives were about to change. Onwards and upwards from here.

CHAPTER 29

"It's mine now"

Mack went to the Heaven's Door night club that evening. The security manager came up to him "hey Mack, haven't seen you for a couple of nights, you OK?" "Yeah" said Mack "I need to have a word, there are going to be some changes from now on". "Oh, what?" "I'll be running the club from now on, Handforth had to go back to Manchester to get away from some heat, we won't be seeing him for a bit." The man whose name was Gary or 'Gaz' said "really? I think I'll give him a call to make sure that this is ok if you don't mind?" "Go ahead" said Mack, "you'll find his phone is turned off, he needs to be out of the picture for a while". Gaz was clearly puzzled "I'm not fucking happy about this, Lee should have told me and I should be running the show, you've only been here two fucking minutes".

Mack saw this could go one of two ways. Either he ended up smacking Gaz or he could see how far he needed to go. "It's this simple Gaz. It's mine now and if you don't like it you can fuck off and if you don't want to fuck off I'll make your mind up for you; so what's it gonna be?" Backed into a corner Gaz considered his options for exactly two seconds. He had seen the dark side of Mack personally and, although he was a handy lad himself he knew a nutter when he saw one. He also knew that genuine paid employment on the coast was like rocking horse shit, impossible to find. "Yeah whatever, but let's get one thing straight; I look after the doors and you run the club. I know the punters here and we have a good thing going on."

"Spot on Gaz, you look after the place for me and I'll see you are looked after. We are going to run a good ship here. And by the way - if you see any cunts dealing heavy shit you let me know"

"You've got it gaffer" Well, that was painless thought Mack. He was used to responsibility, this would give him something to get his teeth into and also suss out any dodgy dealings in the town.

Mack went to the bar and ordered a bottle of *Mahou*. He had a lovely cash nest egg as well as a cosy income, things were falling into place. He would keep things quiet for a while and let things take their natural course. He had created something of a void in the supply chain and inevitably it would be filled by other scum-sucking evil cunts. And inevitably they would come to learn the errors of their ways.

In common with most resort towns Fuengirola had a high season and a not so high season. Being on the Costa del Sol it enjoyed all year round trade due to two factors; climate and golf. Being close to North Africa the climate was considered comfortable throughout the winter months usually being between 16 and 24 degrees. This provided the other factor – golf. Almost nowhere else in the world boasted over fifty high quality golf courses within an hour's drive of each other. A few of these were of international standard such as Valderrama and Sotogrande. There was Gualdalhorce, the home course of Miguel Angel Jimenez and other courses of equal high standard. This attracted hordes of golfers, mostly men enjoying a free drinking pass from their long suffering wives. There were long established companies offering organized golfing holidays and any bar that attracted a group of these free drinking, born again teenagers could boost their takings tremendously.

This additional source of business didn't really affect Mack's night club. During the summer months the club was open until 4:30 AM and during the low season until 3 AM.

During summer Mack would leave locking up to Gaz except for Friday and Saturday night when the takings could be a few thousand Euros. This required a greater degree of security. The club had a state of the art safe and no money left the premises during the night but care was needed to ensure that everything was secured.

So it was that one night the last stragglers had

left and Mack was helping tidy the tables. The big clean-up was taken care of during the day but it just helped to organise things a little before they left. The doors had not yet been locked and suddenly Mack was aware of a commotion at the top of the stairs. He heard Gaz's voice saying "Get out you cunts, we're shut!" He was just about to head upstairs when he saw five Moroccans heading down the stairs. It didn't take much working out what this was about. They clearly thought they were going to dish out some retribution for punishment received.

The five were a mixed bunch. Mack wasn't certain, because they all looked the fucking same to him, but he was in no doubt that at least one of them would be among the two he had sorted out before. Moroccans didn't come in big sizes, they were generally lightly built and under six feet tall and these were no different. However, what they lack in size they made up for in viciousness. They were accustomed to carrying knives and using them without conscience. Three of this lot were carrying mean looking 'zombie' knives, the other two pulled out 18" machetes. They hadn't come to punish Mack; they were here for much more than that. Mack was on a sticky wicket and he knew it. This would need all his abilities; fortunately he was not short on those. Behind the bar was a baseball bat for insurance purposes and Gaz came down the stairs carrying an iron bar kept in the cupboard at the top of the stairs.

One of the Moroccans decided he wanted to give Mack a narrative of why they were there and what they were going to do – first mistake. If you are going to do it, get on with it. They obviously hadn't read rule #1; get in first and get in hard. "You fucking bastard, now you get it!" said one of the filthy cockroaches. He looked like he hadn't washed in a month. He couldn't have been more than ten stone wet through. As intense as the situation was Mack was still amazed at the cocksure attitude of these fuckers. They lived in gangland, they talked gang language, telling each other how hard they were and what they would do to their enemies. They watched too much TV and believed that they could stab and fight in numbers to enforce their will on others.

They could see Mack was more than a match for any one of them but they believed that their superior numbers would be enough. And normally they would be right. The problem was that; in any group there was always a weak member. A hanger-on. Someone who was there to make up the numbers but ultimately did not have the same vicious intent as the leader or leaders. You could spot them a mile off; just a step back from the others. A look of uncertainty in their eyes. It was just beginning to dawn on them that this was not on the TV, This was real and the blood would be for real also. And so it was that the rearmost member of the group, Jaul Jouiti turned tail and ran; not knowing that Gaz had locked the door behind him. Not only that, Gaz was stood behind him and, as he turned, Gaz levelled him by smashing the iron bar straight into his face, followed by an end-game shot to the back of the head. This left four of the cunts and probably only two of which were true nasty fuckers.

Mack leapt over behind the bar which achieved two things; firstly he was out of direct stabbing reach and secondly he had picked up the baseball bat. The wankers would now have to vault the bar or come around to the bar entrance which was typically narrow.

The Moroccans now had Mack behind the bar in front of them, a gang member out of action (properly) and Gaz behind them with an iron bar. Perhaps they should have thought this through a bit more.

Mack could see that Gaz could be in trouble if they turned their attention to him. The Moroccans were looking forwards and backwards not really knowing who to attack first. Just then they did Mack a huge favour. One of them jumped on to the bar, he wasn't athletic or tall enough to vault it. As he stood on the bar to jump down the other side Mack smacked his legs from under him knocking him onto his back and winding him. He didn't have time to catch his breath; Mack piled the baseball bat through his wind pipe followed by a home-run blow that finished his sorry existence. Two down and not even breathing hard.

Gaz was doing a brilliant job; simply hovering round the back of the group so they couldn't focus their attack. One of the skinny arseholes came round to the bar entrance with a machete held out in front of him.

Knives, machetes and swords come under the same category; lethal weapons. At least they should be when wielded correctly. All stabbing implements can only be successful when used with a stabbing motion – a thrust. Swiping and swinging only gives the opponent time to move. If the blade connects clearly it can cause much injury, but if it doesn't then the opponent has a chance to do something about it. Remember it's Mack we are dealing with here. Ice cold and calculating, with lightning reflexes and super focussed responses. The blade slashed, the bat smashed the motherfucker crashed. And then received something he didn't sign on for.

In the background one of the two remaining tossers had turned to watch his colleague attempt to engage Mack. Horrified at what he saw he did not notice Gaz move up behind him and finish his involvement with an iron bar piling through his skull. Gaz was a handy lad but even he had not been in a situation such as this before although he had quickly realized it was an 'us or them' scenario. No time for niceties or trying to calculate how much force to use. No, get in, get it done.

So one low-life left and Mack came out from behind the bar. The last one had a knife but it was the look in his eyes that showed he wouldn't be using it. In fact he threw it to the ground and held his hands up. "Okay, no trouble I go now" The look in his eyes was priceless. Half an hour ago he had been a drug dealing gangster with his gangster buddies planning and laughing how they were going to 'off' the infidel in the club. The club was their patch, no-one told them what to do where they ruled. They would put down a marker and show these 'kuffar' that they were for real. "Let's go" they said, fully confident they were mobhanded and tooled up. They would wait until the club was empty and then go in and do the 'business'. It wasn't supposed to go like this. He was in a gang and he was going with his crew to enforce their territory. They were ruthless, they were invincible, and they could not be beaten. The English fucker would get what was coming to him. No-one would dare touch them after this. They could deal anything they wanted, they could fuck young white girls, they could stab young white boys who said anything. Yeah, this was who they were, the main men. Now they would be kings. Except it had all gone down the pan. There was only supposed to be one white fucker. There were five of them, all tooled up. Now there was only him, Mujahid El Haloui, all 9 stone of him wet through with 30 stone of white menace either side of him. "They made me come, I not want to do this" was what he started to say. You know how this goes, all he managed was "they made me…." Mack smashed him in the face with the baseball bat whilst Gaz pummelled him round the back of the head with the iron bar. No contest really, but they both knew what would have happened if the Moroccan cunts had got the upper hand. There would be pieces of Mack all over the club (He would never know what they *actually* planned to do). They would be swaggering back to their pit, shoulders swaying looking at anyone and challenging them with their eyes to say something, anything so they would show them who was boss. Well they weren't the boss, they were nothing. Apart from being dead they would no longer peddle their filth around Fuengirola, they would no longer bother young white girls from Hemel Hempstead or Richmond, they would no longer gather around white boys acting all cocky and threatening or even cutting them. It was over for them and their worthless existence. The pit they had sunken into had collapsed around them and buried them.

Mack started to breathe again and said to Gaz, "I'll nip home and get the car, get them to the bottom of the stairs; we'll have to decide what to do with them". It was already getting light outside and a few clubbers, all the worse for wear took no notice of Mack as he hurried through the back streets to get his car. It was already 23 degrees, today would be a hot one. Mack was already forming a plan. One of the main advantages of the Costa del Sol was the sea. It was the ideal place to dispose of the scumbags. The problem was, this time of year, where to find a spot with no-one around, but he had an idea.

Driving back to the club he was pleased to find that Gaz had wrapped all the bodies in black bin bags. Hopefully it would look like they were taking out the trash - which they were.

There was still hardly anyone around as they loaded the bodies into the Audi. With the back seats down they just managed to fit them all in. All bagged up they no longer had to look at the smashed up heads and faces of the filthy scum.

Gaz was looking a bit pale and Mack said to him "I can't thank you enough mate. That could have been a real problem." "Yeah I know" said Gaz "I've been in some scrapes but that was fucking intense, how do you keep so calm?" "That's only on the outside" said Mack "inside I was fucking shitting myself. I know I can handle myself but without you there I would have been toast". Gaz actually managed a joke "you wouldn't have been toast mate, you would have been fucking mincemeat!" They both laughed out loud with a release of tension. The last half an hour had been an experience neither of them would forget in their lifetimes. It also forged a bond between the two that would grow to become a lifelong friendship.

Now, what to do? The problem was that they needed to dispose of the rubbish quick. At this time of the day the Guardia Civil would be on the lookout for drink-drivers and they could be stopped for no reason. Even if they were stopped for no reason and were not alcohol positive, the Guardia had a habit of *always* searching a vehicle. They just liked the power trip.

There were two areas Mack would have liked to get to. One, past Algeciras, going round past Tarifa, the coast was virtually deserted with lots of beaches with no-one around. The other one, and favourite, was the other way up past Nerja where the coast turned into cliffs plunging down to the sea. This had to be the way thought Mack. The A7 now had a bypass around Málaga, the traffic would be heavier and they would be on four and five lane motorways where they would blend in better.

So Mack set off up the Carretera de Mijas to pick up the AP7 toll road to Málaga keeping to a steady 120Kph. This road didn't touch the large city of Málaga and swept round keeping inland from the coast past Rincon de la Victoria and Velez Malaga and shooting past Nerja following the signs for Motril. At Nerja you could continue on the *Autovia* or come off onto the old N340 and take the cliff road towards Almuñecar on the Costa Tropical.

Almuñecar was one of Mack's favourite places to visit and he had been with Jill only a couple of weekends ago. This wasn't a pleasure trip however.

As you wound your way around the meandering coast road it rose and followed the cliffs which gave a spectacular view of the Mediterranean hundreds of feet below. To enjoy the view even better, from time to time there were places to pull off called *miradors* literally Spanish for 'lookout'. Because most of the traffic nowadays kept on the motorway the coast road had almost no traffic on it. The Spanish working day started at 10am and before this it was almost deserted. Mack waited until the cliffs had risen high enough and pulled over onto a *mirador.* In both directions he could see the road coming around the cliffs. He waited until there was no chance of a car that had been out of sight coming around the corner and then he and Gaz jumped out of the car, opened the boot and took about thirty panicked seconds launching the bodies as far as they could over the cliff edge. Before they did they had the unenviable task of removing the black bags which would carry prints and such. He didn't care how far the bodies flew over the cliffs, in an ideal world they would reach the sea and never be seen again. Even if they landed down the rocks, the chances of them being seen would be slim and the gulls would take care of most of the flesh. Mack had a moment where he had to push the image to the back of his mind with a small shudder.

"Come on Gaz, let's get the fuck out of here". Gaz

needed no persuading they jumped back in the car and set off back to Fuengirola. On the way they stopped and gathered the black bags and screwed them up into another bag as tight as possible and deposited them in a nearby waste bin. No-one would thing twice as to what the bags had contained. They then ran the car through the car wash and used the pay-per-minute vacuum cleaner to clean the boot and the rest of the car.

Mack dropped Gaz off in town with a man hug and knowing wink. Neither of them would ever speak of this again, even to each other. It wouldn't be good conversation and these memories were best left where they were. The truth was; neither of them were cold-blooded killers. However given the circumstances there had been no option. Mack felt nothing for filth such as they had been. Not for Lee Handforth or Vlad/Piotr/Pete or their crews. These people chose their path in life and would run their own risks accordingly. No, he wasn't a cold-blooded killer but he had his own mission, his own drives and his own agenda. Inevitably, if these motherfucking scum were to be deprived of their living, their income and their total lack of morals, they would need to be deprived of their lives.....

Mack went home to bed.